GOING THE DISTANCE

Stephanie Perry Moore
&
Derrick Moore

GOING THE DISTANCE

Alec London Series
Book 3

MOODY PUBLISHERS
CHICAGO

© 2012 by
STEPHANIE PERRY MOORE
AND DERRICK MOORE

Edited by Kathryn Hall
Interior design: Ragont Design
Cover design: TS Design Studio
Cover photo and illustrations: TS Design Studio and 123rf.com

Library of Congress Cataloging-in-Publication Data

Moore, Stephanie Perry.
    Going the distance / Stephanie Perry Moore, Derrick C. Moore.
        p. cm. — (Alec London series ; bk. #3)
    Summary: Alec faces challenges over the summer when his father enrolls him in baseball camp and his nemesis from school shows up, but things start to improve when his family goes to Los Angeles to visit their mother, who is working in Hollywood, until he is once again brought up short. Educational exercises provided at the end of each chapter.
    ISBN 978-0-8024-0412-1
    [1. Family problems--Fiction. 2. Christian life--Fiction. 3. African Americans—Fiction.] I. Moore, Derrick C. II. Title.
PZ7.M788125Gnv 2012
[Fic]—dc23

                                                                    2011028976

Printed by Bethany Press in Bloomington, MN - 01/2012

1 3 5 7 9 10 8 6 4 2

Printed in the United States of America

To our youngest daughter
Sheldyn Ashli Moore

We were surprised and excited when we
learned you were on the way.
God truly blessed us with the gift of you, our doll baby.
We're so proud of you working extra hard in school.
All of that effort landed you on the National
Jr. Honor Society this year.
We know that if you and every reader continue
to go the distance and never give up . . .
excellence can be achieved!
Sheldyn, keep hitting your goals out
of the park—we love you!

Contents

In Charge

1

"Okay, class, so listen up. Three more events to go and the fourth grade can win Field Day! Remember, every one of you will get a ticket to Six Flags. We can do this, class," said Mr. Wade. I could tell how much he wanted our class to win.

"Now, it's time for the three-legged race. Tyrod, Alec, I need my strongest guys to back up the team," our teacher continued.

Trey called out, "Why do you think they're the toughest and the strongest? *I* just won the sack hop. Whatever . . . I don't wanna race with Tyrod anyway. My foot and his foot tied together. No way!"

"Your feet aren't gonna be tied together," Morgan called out to Trey. My friends Morgan and Trey were always competing with each other about something. Now she wanted to point out that he didn't know everything. "Your ankles will be tied together, not your feet," she corrected him.

"Whatever," Trey responded. "I don't wanna be tied to him."

This wasn't going right. The whole class started arguing back and forth. It's like nobody was keeping the bigger prize in mind. First-place team wins Six Flags tickets! Didn't they just hear Mr. Wade? Didn't they want to win? The title was almost ours. But even though we were in first place, one of the other three teams could still beat us.

As if Mr. Wade were reading my mind, he called out, "Listen! You all are getting off track! Didn't you just hear me? Six Flags tickets for the winners! Plus, I really want us to win. This is my first year as a fourth grade teacher. The other teachers talk about competing at Field Day all year long. So, do it for me! Come on, guys, didn't we have a good school year?"

"All you did was yell all the time and scream at us," Tyrod mumbled.

Hearing that remark, Mr. Wade immediately responded. "No, I stayed on you guys. And all of you, including you, Tyrod, passed the CRCT standard test. So, I'd say we had a great year. Yeah, I might have been tough on the class, but that's because I care."

About a month ago, if you had asked me if I thought Mr. Wade cared, I would have told you no way. Tyrod was at least right about the fact that every time we turned around Mr. Wade was fussing about something.

He even took me to the office a couple of times. And that was the last place I wanted to go because my dad is the assistant principal. That means I got into trouble at school and at home. But then our teacher pulled me aside and told me that he thought I was bright and had a lot of potential. He told me the reason he was on my back all the time was because he didn't want me to take shortcuts. He pointed out that going the distance is what's important. Mr. Wade helped me know that hard work pays off in the end. And, believe me, the whole fourth grade year wasn't an easy one for me.

For one thing, it was the first year that my mom wasn't home with us. Besides the fact that she and my dad were having problems, Mom is an actress with a television show out in California. When she first gave us the news that she was leaving, Mom didn't think she'd be there long. Although she had come back for a short visit, the whole year was going by and she still wasn't home for good.

I really miss her and can't wait until she comes back to stay. You see, there's way too much stuff going on with my older brother, Antoine. Sometimes I wish he wasn't my older brother at all. When it comes to sports, we're very competitive with each other. At times, I do a whole lot better than him and that causes tension between us.

On top of it all, this was also the first year my father has been working at my school. At the beginning of the year, kids teased me for being the assistant principal's son. But that didn't mean my dad treated me like I'm special. In fact, he was super hard on me. He told me it was because he has high hopes for me. Dad always gives me pretty much the same message as my teacher. They both say how it's important to give my all in everything I do. It's called "going the distance."

Because I'm so competitive, I really want to win Field Day. It's a big end-of-the-year fun activity, and the big prize makes it even more worth it. Actually, if there wasn't something cool at stake, I'd still want us to be the winning team. I just want to be the best. But it's not just up to me. If our class wants to win, we have to get focused.

So everyone could hear me, I shouted out, "Quit trippin', everybody! Let's do this! We're almost there! Come on!"

"Hey, don't act like you're our leader or somethin'," Tyrod said crossly, as he stepped in front of me. "I don't wanna be tied to you and I'm not racing with you. If I'm your partner and we win, you're just gonna say it's because you did it. So, you need to run with your little friend, Trey. When y'all trip and fall, you'll wish I was your partner."

Mr. Wade looked straight at the guy who was getting on my nerves. "Tyrod! You don't get to decide who'll be partners! I'm running this. Shavon and Lacey, you go first. Gilmer and Trey, you go next. Tyrod and Alec, you bring it home."

As soon as Mr. Wade tied our bandanas and walked away, Tyrod bent down and loosened ours.

"That's gonna come off," I said.

"Well, it can't be as tight as he made it."

"What's your problem, man?"

"What's your problem?!" Tyrod shot back at me.

"I'm tryin' to win. I don't have a problem." Then, I paused and added, "Well, I guess I do. You're my problem."

We were so busy fussing that we didn't even know the race had started. There's no doubt about it, we aren't friends. When it was our turn to take off running, we were still arguing and didn't move.

Mr. Wade called out, "Boys! Quiet! Now, go!"

At first, our class was in the lead. But, because Tyrod and I had wasted precious time, the other teams were gaining on us. Then it happened. The bandana holding us together wasn't tight enough, and it soon came apart. The other teams quickly passed us by. Before we knew it, we were disqualified.

Mr. Wade was not happy. "Boys! What happened? I tied that bandana tight; how'd it come loose?"

Tyrod tried to blame me, but Mr. Wade wasn't hearing it. The other kids in our class were mad too because now we were in second place.

It was time for the basketball toss. A team of four people from each class has fifty seconds, and the class with the most baskets wins. When it was our turn, we were all pushing and shoving each other. The time was quickly winding down and we didn't have any baskets. We were now in third place.

Before the last event, Mr. Wade took us all over by the big oak tree so we could rest. As we sat underneath the tree drinking water and cooling off, he told us, "You guys don't seem interested in going to Six Flags."

"Yes, we are!" Trey and some of the kids yelled out.

"Well then, act like you're competing for something.

13

Put your heart into it and give it all you've got. Even if it's not about winning the prize, it should be about doing your best," Mr. Wade reminded us.

"What does our heart have to do with this?" Tyrod asked, trying to challenge Mr. Wade.

"By that, I mean it's about your character. You guys were all excited and looking forward to Field Day. You have to remember that every time you compete, it's about going the distance. It's almost over, and you should want to finish strong. You already passed the CRCT, and you did well academically. Now, you're ready to go on to the fifth grade. You made the grade with the books, and you can do the same thing with sports. If you learn how to go the distance and finish strong, it will be a trait you can carry for the rest of your life. Even when things get in your way, you can go on out there and win. So, let's do this!"

Mr. Wade lined us up for the tug of war game and made me the anchor. Tyrod didn't like that, so he wouldn't pull. It was no surprise that because we didn't work together, we didn't win. But we were all disappointed anyway.

"If I would've been at the back, we would've won," Tyrod said, trying to get under my skin.

I was so glad that this was the last day of school and I wouldn't have to see him for the rest of the summer. Tyrod always talked a lot of junk. But if he would've pulled his weight, then maybe we could've won.

It didn't get any better when a couple of the other teachers came up to Mr. Wade and teased him about losing.

"Sorry, guy. Hope things work out for you next time!" one teacher said with a quick laugh.

"You didn't think you were going to come to the fourth grade in your first year and claim the Field Day prize, did you?" asked another teacher.

"Okay, go on and talk about me. I can take it. Next year, I hope my class will work harder and win," Mr. Wade said to the other teachers.

Then he called the class together one more time and said, "I just want you guys to understand that being tough isn't about having a lot to say or flexing your muscles. Don't forget, it's about your heart and your character. You didn't give me your all today. You didn't give each other what you needed either. Every one of you guys needs to look deep inside. I know it's been a tough fourth grade year. There was a lot of material to learn, but you did it. Now go on and make your fifth grade year even better. If you ever need to talk, I'll be right down the hall. Remember, I'll be there for you. Have a good summer."

Morgan and the other girls in our class rushed up to Mr. Wade and gave him hugs. The guys just looked on, taking it all in—even Tyrod. It seemed like everyone was thinking the same thing. If we could go back and do those last few events over again, we would give it our all for Mr. Wade. He was right. We would have to remember his words from now on. People with character don't quit. People with heart endure to the end and finish strong.

● ● ●

"The house looks real nice, Dad. Mom's going to be so surprised," I said to my father as we finished decorating. We were getting ready for my mom's birthday and homecoming celebration all rolled into one.

"What time does her plane land? What time is she supposed to get here? Do we have to pick her up, or is she takin' a taxi?" my brother asked, just as excited as I was.

"Andre, son, I must admit you've got the house lookin' mighty nice. Your missus is going to be very happy," Grandma said to my father. She was letting us know we had done a good job of cleaning our home.

"Tell me, Dad . . . what time is she comin'?" Antoine asked again, unable to hold back his excitement.

Dad patted him on the shoulder and said, "Calm down, son, I know you're anxious to see her. She's not supposed to arrive for another couple of hours. A car service is bringing her home, so all we have to do is wait."

Grandma started sniffing like she was trying to detect something. "I don't smell anything. What about the food? Who's cookin'?" she asked with a knowing smile.

The three of us didn't say a word. We just gathered around her with sad eyes and pitiful faces. We needed her help. She knew we were trying to ask her to fix something.

"I guess y'all like my cubed steak, yellow rice, greens, and cornbread. I can cook that up."

"Well, you know it. Come on, Mama, let me take you

shopping. Lisa will be here in a little while." Dad grabbed his keys, Grandma got her purse, and out the door they went.

"Okay, so you know we need to get along," Antoine said to me when we were alone.

I just looked at him because I wasn't the one who got our rough cousin to beat him up. No, he did that to me. Sure, he felt bad about it later on. But, I was never really sure if Antoine was done with causing problems between us.

"You're the one who had an issue with me," I said to Antoine.

"I'm past all that. You forgive me, right?"

I did forgive him, but it hurt that things even came to that. Some nights I still remembered getting a bloody nose when Lil' Pete threw a basketball at my face. The only thing worse was finding out that my own brother told him to do it. That was harder to swallow than having a bad sore throat.

But Antoine was right. We didn't need to be arguing and carrying on when Mom came home. Everything needed to be peaceful. Nice and fun.

Antoine stuck out his hand and said, "Truce?"

I figured I'd let the past be the past. So I stuck out my hand and shook his. It was important for Mom to come home to a stress-free place.

Then I got an idea. I took a piece of pink construction paper and some crayons and went outside. I sat down on the curb and tried to think of what I could say on a card for Mom. Just thinking about her coming home after all this time, I wanted to cry. But I wanted to be strong for her even more.

"What are you doing?" I heard a familiar voice say. I looked up and saw it was my friend Morgan.

"Hey," I said, surprised and happy to see her. "I'm makin' a card."

"Yeah, it looks like that's what you're supposed to be doing, but . . . uh, the paper is blank."

"I know," I replied. "My mom is comin' home today, and I wanna say something super special. This is a happy time, and I don't wanna write anything sad. I don't wanna put somethin' down that doesn't mean anything either." Then I let out a sigh and said, "I just don't know what to say."

Morgan got off her bike and stooped down to dust off a spot on the curb. Then she sat down next to me. *Man,* I thought as I watched her, *It's just a little dirt.* It's not like it was gonna hurt her or anything.

"Just speak from your heart. Have you prayed about it?" she asked.

I shook my head and Morgan didn't waste any time. She grabbed my hand and prayed, "Lord, please bless Alec. He's real excited about his mom coming home. He's trying to write her a special card. Please give him the words to say. We love You and we thank You. Amen."

I added, "Amen."

"Maybe after you finish with your card you can ride with me. I'm going around the block four times."

"How do you know it's going to take me that long to think of something?"

Morgan said, "See, that's not what I meant. You shouldn't think negatively. Remember, what I always say—keep a positive attitude."

I laughed at that, knowing she was just messing with me. But, she did have a point too. Just as she took off, I closed my eyes and started thinking about what I wanted to say.

When Dad and Grandma came back from shopping, I was still working on it. A little while later, I finally finished and placed my card on the table next to the cake. I thought it looked pretty good. As soon as Antoine saw it, he wanted to make one too. But it didn't take him long to write his and it wasn't on construction paper. He just ripped a piece of notebook paper out of his book and wrote, "Mom, I'm glad you're home." Dad and I just looked at him.

Folding it over, he put the pitiful card next to mine. "Mom doesn't care. She just wants to know how I feel. This is good," said Antoine.

Just then I noticed Dad pacing back and forth. Mom was supposed to have arrived by now. Another hour went by, and we were still waiting for her to show up. I could tell Dad was getting worried. Grandma had finished cooking and had gone over to her sister's house. So the three of us were left wondering when Mom would come.

Then Dad's cell phone rang. He hurried to pick it up and quickly said, "It's your mom. I'm sure she's just running late."

But as their conversation went on, Antoine and I stood watching him. We could tell it wasn't good news. Dad paced back and forth for a few more minutes, huffing and shaking his head over and over again. It seemed like it was taking forever for him to finish talking.

"Guys, I've got some bad news and some good news," Dad said when he finally laid his phone on the table.

Antoine spoke first. "She's not comin' home."

Dad went on to explain, "No, the network picked up their show. In addition to the eight episodes they finished taping, they want to tape eight more."

"So the bad news is, she's not coming," I added. "What's the good news?"

"She asked if we could come out there in July. That's pretty good, right? Spending some time as a family in Hollywood sounds good to me," Dad said, trying to sound upbeat.

I looked down at the floor and Antoine looked away.

"Aw, come on, boys," Dad said, trying to keep us encouraged. "We can do this. The time will go by quickly, you'll see. Before you know it, we'll head out to California and stay with your mom for a whole month. Then maybe after that she'll be coming home for good."

In spite of Dad trying to stay on a positive note, this was hard news to take. I wanted to take the cake and toss it across the room. I wanted to take my card and rip it to shreds. I wanted to take the decorations and tear them down, but I knew that wouldn't change things. Besides, this wasn't just hard on me. Dad and Antoine were sad too. Right then I decided I was going to try if Dad was willing to try.

Somehow finding the strength, I said, "This is gonna be okay."

"Yeah," said Antoine. Surprisingly, he was being tough too. Letting out a big sigh, he said, "Hollywood here we come!"

● ● ●

"Alec? Hey, baby, I'm so sorry I'm not there," Mom said when I answered her call.

"I'm sorry you're not here too, Mom, but Dad talked to us. We ate your cake and Grandma cooked us a good meal. So I'm okay . . . and . . . happy birthday!"

"Thank you, Alec. It really means a lot to me to hear you sound so positive. Mommy would be there if I could."

"I know, Mom. My friend Morgan talks all the time about how good the premier was when we saw your show. She wants to be an actress one day. I don't know why she thinks acting is so cool. Anyway, I'm glad you guys got more episodes; and Dad said we're going to come out there in July."

"Yep, for a whole month. I can't wait," she said happily.

"Me too. Where are we gonna fit?" I asked, remembering how small her place was.

"I know, right? Well, I've gotten rid of the studio apartment," she said with a little laugh. "I've moved into a two-bedroom condo, so it'll be enough room for all of us."

"That means I'll have to share a room with Antoine?"

"Don't worry. Your room has twin beds," she said. "Plus, I thought you two worked out your differences."

"Yeah, we have," I said quickly. I didn't want there to be any issues that would keep her from wanting us to come.

"So, what are you going to do for the rest of June?" she asked.

"Well, the pool opens tomorrow. Remember when you took me to the YMCA for swim lessons?"

"Yeah, you learned pretty quickly. For someone your age, you had one of the best backstrokes the instructor had ever seen."

"Well, I'm just excited about going to the new pool and having a chance to get some swim time. It'll feel great to relax. I mean, I'm still gonna do some studying on the Internet and everything. I'll be learning new words and reading some of the books on the summer reading list. But, mostly I'm gonna chill, Mom, until we come out there to California."

"Now, that does sound good. And when you come to L.A., we'll go to the beach in Malibu. We couldn't go when you came for Christmas because there wasn't enough time, but you're going to love it. And I've got some special people I want you to meet. You know, I grew up here."

"Yes, ma'am, you were born there," I said. That's about all I knew about it because she never talked much about her family. "I'm happy that the three of us are coming to see you, Mom."

"Well, in the meantime, keep writing me those letters. They get me through. Now, put your brother on the phone for me. Love you."

"Yes, ma'am. I love you too."

After Antoine took the phone, I got on my knees and prayed, "Lord, today is my mom's birthday and although we're not spending it together, I know we're together because she is in my heart. Thank You for helping me to realize that it's not totally a bad thing that we're apart from Mom. My whole family's going out there in July. This could be the best thing that's happened to us. Oh, and thank You, Lord, for taking care of my mom so far away. I love You. Amen."

Early the next morning, Dad woke us up. He wanted Antoine and me to ride with him through Stone Mountain Park.

"Dad, it's too early in the morning," Antoine complained. "This is our summer break and we wanna go to the pool a little later. Can we can ride our bikes through Stone Mountain another time?" He was definitely speaking for both of us.

"Boys, did you guys think you were going to do whatever you want to all summer? Your grandma and your aunt are going to visit your uncle in Alabama for a couple weeks. I'm off today, but most days I'll still be working at school."

"It's the summer. Why do you have to work?" Antoine asked.

"I'm the assistant principal all year long. I don't get a break. Besides that, I'm not going to just leave you boys home alone all day."

Antoine said, "I'm in middle school! I can take care of things around here!"

"You and your brother have been fussing off and on this whole school year."

"Yeah, but we'll be okay, Dad. I promise we don't need a babysitter or anything," I jumped in and said.

"I'm not saying you need a babysitter, but I'm not leaving you here either. You boys need to be up doing something positive. So I put you in a summer camp. I'll be able to drop you off and pick you up afterward."

"A camp? Dad, I need a break from learning!" Antoine said forcefully.

"That comment makes no sense. You never need a break from learning. Even when you reach my age you should continue to learn."

"But I don't need a big education, Dad. I'm going to the sports league," said Antoine.

"Son, I don't want to kill your dreams. You're a great athlete, but everyone needs a backup plan. Even if you play in the NBA, you still need to train for something else. Besides, someday you'll retire when you finish with your career. If you're fortunate enough to make a lot of money, you'll need to be able to manage it. Only a solid education can teach you how to do that. Now come on, the bikes are loaded up. Let's go."

Stone Mountain Park was nice, but I probably would have cared more about it if it wasn't seven o'clock in the morning. Then, once we started on the path and woke up a bit, we enjoyed it.

When we got to the top of the mountain and looked out over Georgia, Dad said, "Boys, I know it's been a rough year for you. It's been hard not having your mom here. You guys are growing up, and you've had your differences. Plus, I've pushed you to take on more responsibility with keeping the house clean. With all of that going on, I want you to know that I'm proud of you. I know you're also getting applause from heaven."

"What does that mean?" asked Antoine.

"That means God is proud of you too. I remember when I was your age. When things didn't go the way I wanted them to, I had to learn that I could still make the best of every day. You can always take something sour and make it sweet!"

"So what kind of camp are we going to?" asked Antoine. Neither one of us was convinced that it was the right thing to do.

"Come on," Dad said, as we followed him back down the hill.

When we got to the car, Dad hitched the bicycles on the back. He took out a baseball and gloves and started tossing around the ball.

"You mean, we're going to a baseball camp?"

"You've got it. Isn't that going to be fun?"

"No way. I'm not goin' to no baseball camp," Antoine protested.

Although my brother was being rude, I wanted to say, *Me neither, Dad. Neither one of us likes baseball.* If he would have said football or basketball, we'd have been okay with it. But baseball . . . well, it just wasn't our sport.

"Listen here, young man, you're not going to tell me what you're not going to do. Camp starts on Monday, and you will be there. Plus, we're all going to church tomorrow. I am the man of this family, I run the show. I know what's best for you guys, and you all are going. That's final."

Dad was a little angry that we weren't excited about his plan. He took the ball and gloves and tossed them into the trunk of the car and told us to get in.

Antoine didn't like the idea about playing baseball and neither did I. But it didn't take long to find out that what we wanted didn't matter. We were going to camp because our dad had laid down the law. His plan was the one we were going to go with because he was still in charge.

Letter to Mom

Dear Mom,

We lost the field day event because the class couldn't get along. At first we were happy that we were winning, but when the tension took over and arguments broke out, we were disqualified.

Even worse than that, I had to endure another letdown. When I thought you were coming home, I was so excited that I made you a card. But when we got the news that you weren't coming home right away, I had to make the best of it. Being me is still tough.

Your son,
Disappointed Alec

GOING THE DISTANCE

Word Search: Baseball Terms

At any baseball game—little league, middle school, high school, college, or pros—find the terms below that are often used.

```
N E G N L T X A V F J C
D A J K U V C Y M I P L
P I T C H R K V Y O B E
I Z A L U X E F J F F A
F K S M C F B M S R J N
F C L E O N U P O K P U
R U Y I I N U E K H X P
E D S Y B A D Q S W B S
L M W A K H R M A U U M
A A L E R F Y W H Y N V
Y R E T T A B E M O T O
Z S W Y O N L F P E T E
```

BATTERY   BUNT   CLEANUP   DIAMOND

HOMERUN   PITCH   RELAY
(Home Run)

28

Can't
Quit

2

"**Dad, do we** have to go to baseball camp?" Antoine asked, after we got up early Monday morning.

Antoine looked over at me and motioned for me to jump into the conversation. He wanted me to help convince Dad we didn't need to go. Really, we just wanted to sleep in. It had been a long time since my brother and I agreed on anything. Whenever I wanted burgers, he wanted hot dogs. If I wanted to watch a basketball game, he wanted to watch wrestling. If I asked for vanilla ice cream, he wanted chocolate. Bottom line: we just didn't agree.

Today was different, though. We both wanted to chill. We both needed our dad to change his mind.

I had to think of something in a flash, so I said, "Hey, Dad, the best dad in the whole wide world . . . your pancakes . . . mmm. I can't wait to eat them. By the way—"

"Yes, Alec?" Dad stopped me before I could even get out what I really wanted to say. "Would this little 'being nice' routine have anything to do with me changing my mind about baseball camp? If so, you can forget about it."

"But, Dad!" I said, stomping my foot. I was angrier than ever.

"Boy, please. I'm not even trying to hear that," he said, looking at me with a steady, strong glare. He didn't even blink. "The answer is final. You're going to this camp. And if the two of you give anyone at the camp any trouble, you're going to wish you hadn't."

"But why, Dad? Why do we have to go? I know you said so, but with no disrespect, we just wanna relax," Antoine said, still pleading our case.

After a long pause, Dad said, "Baseball is a great sport. I played it when I was your age."

"Yeah, but that was a billion years ago, Dad," Antoine said, not helping our cause.

Dad didn't even get upset about that not-so-smart comment. He just laughed and shook his head. I guess he had to agree that it was a long time ago, and a lot has changed. For example, when our dad was young, they didn't have cell phones.

As far as I could tell, he had to know that the things that made up his childhood are now extinct! Whatever he did over the summer when he was our age didn't matter to us. Nowadays, we want a real vacation.

"Baseball is America's game," he told us. "I want you boys to experience good things. I'm not saying that I want you to play major league baseball, but I do want you to at least enjoy this camp. I have a lot of respect for the coach too."

An hour later, Dad dropped us off and drove away. The great coach he had bragged about was already barking orders.

"Quit looking at me! You boys drop down and give me twenty, right now! I'm going to get you in shape before this is over."

The five boys who got there before us were already doing sit-ups. It looked to me like they were out of breath and about to pass out. I didn't think we were ready for this. This was only the warm-up. If we didn't get practice right, did we even have a chance at playing the game?

I looked over at Antoine, and he was shaking his head. In a low voice, I heard him say, "Oh, man! There's Jelani."

"It's cool. Don't even worry about him," I said to Antoine. I knew he felt bad about acting tough with Jelani in basketball earlier in the year. Now he didn't want to face him.

But I quickly found out that I spoke too soon to my big brother. Right after I encouraged him, my mouth almost dropped to the ground. There was Tyrod! This day was going to be worse than I thought!

The coach was trying to wear us out. He made us run three miles, do a lot of stretching, and a bunch of other exercises.

"I hear a whole lot of groaning, and I'm not up for it. Let me introduce myself. I'm Coach Riley, and I don't play.

Your parents sent you to me this summer because they know you're in good hands, and you'll get good training. I don't babysit, so if you thought you could get away with whining like babies, just know this is the wrong place. I'm not the one to whine around."

"Excuse me. I thought this was supposed to be a fun camp," Tyrod spoke up boldly. He was ready to be difficult as usual.

"Young man, you need to raise your hand. When I call on you, then you can speak. Yes, we will have fun if everyone acts right. Now, for talking out of turn, drop down and give me twenty push-ups."

Tyrod frowned and hesitated. "But I didn't know your rules."

Coach "No Nonsense" Riley groaned and said, "Okay, now make it thirty. Got anything else to say?"

I couldn't hold back a chuckle. That's just the kind of treatment that Tyrod needed. Then, before I knew it, Coach Riley came and stood in front of me.

"Funny man, join him. Thirty for you too."

The two of us went over to the side. I didn't even say anything to Tyrod. I just knew this camp thing was going to be even worse than I imagined. Not only was I not going to have my mom with me for a while, I had to put up with Tyrod. Ugh! I can't even catch a break!

I could tell we were in for a long haul, so I prayed, *"Lord, help me to get along with others and treat people the way You want me to. Even though I forgave Tyrod for being mean to me in the fourth grade, he still doesn't get it. I don't want to see him in the fifth grade, much less this summer. Since I have no choice but to deal with him, help me to stay calm before I say something that I truly will regret. Amen."*

● ● ●

Finally, it's our chance to enjoy the new community pool! The sun was shining brightly, and our entire neighborhood was having a special pool party in honor of Father's Day. I was pumped up and ready to have some fun.

"Y'all ready?" Dad asked, wearing the ugliest swim trunks I've ever seen. They were covered with stripes and polka dots in every color of the rainbow.

Antoine was laughing so hard that he had to grab his chest and gasp for air. I was in shock, not knowing which was worse—his trunks or the straw hat that Dad was wearing. It was the size of a big Mexican sombrero.

"What? I don't look cool?"

"If that was the look you were going for, Dad, you really messed up," I said.

"Well, these are the only ones I have," said Dad, pointing at his trunks.

"Yeah, we know," Antoine said, as he shoved a box at him.

"Pops, open this. Last week, Grandma took us shopping, and we bought you a few things for Father's Day. When we told her that the pool was opening, she said we should get you some new swimwear."

Dad ripped the box open, and he grinned from ear to ear. He's a big fan of the Falcons. To his surprise, there was a pair of long, black trunks with a red stripe and the Falcon's logo going up the sides. "Oh, boys, thanks . . . this is what's up!"

"Open mine, Dad," I said in a hurry, as I passed him my gift. When he opened the box and put on the pair of sunglasses, he definitely looked way cooler than before.

"This is great! But, you guys didn't have to get me anything."

"Wait! We got you one more thing. This is from both of us," Antoine said, handing Dad his last present.

It brought tears to his eyes to see a brand-new Bible with his name "Dr. Andre London" engraved on the front in gold letters.

"Wow. Now this is special," he said in a serious tone.

"We're proud of you, Dad," Antoine said. "Sometimes it scares me when I think I won't excel in education because you set the bar so high. I don't know. I just don't wanna fail, and I don't wanna disappoint you."

"Son, don't you ever feel like you have to compare yourself to me. As long as you're trying and you're giving your all, I know you're going to succeed. Just don't lower your own bar because you're scared you can't jump over it. There were times when I was younger when I was completely off track and should have been focused. When the recession hit and I lost my job, I wasn't prepared with a backup plan. I'm glad you're proud of me, but when you give 100 percent and have the right attitude, you'll go far. What do you want to be when you grow up?"

We just stared at him, listening hard. This was such a serious conversation. Yeah, we wanted to get to the pool. But we just froze in our tracks with our towels, goggles, and beach ball in hand. The thing about it is, I'm only in elementary school. I haven't been thinking about what or who I want to be. My brother is two years older than me, so maybe he had something in mind. But he looked just as clueless as me.

"I challenge you guys to take a good look at yourselves this summer. I know you're young, but if you don't have any goals or ambitions, then what are you striving for? I mean, I know you both desire to play pro sports. However, the odds aren't in your favor. So think about what drives you. What motivates you? What other interests do you have?"

"I like sports, and I watch ESPN all the time. Maybe I could be on TV as a commentator or something," Antoine said.

"That's great. With all the cable channels and TV shows that they have now, you could own your own sports network. I'm sure your mom would really like that. Alec, what about you?"

"I like to argue my point and fight for what I believe in. But I don't know."

"That sounds like you could be a great attorney. Maybe even a Supreme Court justice someday. Anad remember, the most important thing is to keep the Bible close to our hearts. If we all get in God's Word and obey Him, we'll be on the right course. Together we can ask the Lord to give you boys a plan to help you achieve your goals."

"I love you, Dad," Antoine said, as he reached over and hugged our father.

"I love you, too, man. You both are going to be great men someday. Come here, Alec," Dad said, as he rubbed my head and gave me a hug.

Twenty minutes later when we pulled up to the pool parking lot, it was full of cars.

I asked, "Do all of these people live here? There's no place to park."

When we first moved into the area, there were only a few families. A while ago, I heard Dad say there were over fifty.

As we kept driving until we finally found a space, Dad explained, "The pool area is only for residents in the subdivision. That's why there are only so many spaces. But it'll be all right."

"The pool looks crowded too," I said.

"Go on in," Dad told us, after he finished parking the car.

I was feeling good because our father was with us and we just had a meaningful conversation. He made us believe that we're going to be someone important someday and that felt awesome.

It was good to spend time talking to Dad, but I kind of

wished we could have gotten there sooner. When we walked into the pool area, all of the chairs were taken. A few minutes later, Morgan's stepdad called everyone to eat. Antoine and I were glad because most of the people were coming out while we were jumping in.

When I came up from diving, I was surprised by the sight as I took it all in. I couldn't help but feel a little sad too. There were all these families huddled together. Mothers were drying off their little kids. Husbands were hugging their wives. We were the only ones there who weren't a complete family, and it didn't feel good. My brother didn't seem to care. He just kept splashing around and swimming until Dad called him out and told him to dry off and get a plate.

When Morgan looked my way, I was feeling bad. It was like I'd stepped into an ant bed or something. She came over and said, "Aren't you gonna get somethin' to eat?"

"No, thanks." I was hungry, but my appetite had gone away. Although I just wanted her to go away, Morgan knew me too well.

"What's wrong, Alec?"

I let it out. "Everyone is havin' so much fun with their families, except for me. Okay? My family is split apart, and it's hard to watch. Can't I be upset about it?"

"You can, but not today. It's Father's Day, not Mother's Day. And you have your dad sitting right over there. Be thankful and enjoy that. My stepdad is here, but my father's gone back on the Navy ship, sailing who knows where. I wish I could be with my dad. So quit trippin'."

● ● ●

The tough conversation Morgan had with me really sank into my brain, as if it were a sponge. She was right. My dad was in my life every day. It was okay if I wanted things to be perfect, but I needed to be thankful for all that was right in front of me. So for the rest of the time at the pool, I made up my mind that I would enjoy my dad. That night when we returned home, I whipped up a special milkshake for him.

The next morning, he didn't even have to tell me it was time to get up. I woke up bright and early to make him breakfast.

"What is this?" asked Dad. He came into the kitchen looking surprised.

"Waffles for you, Dad," I replied, as I pulled out the chair for him to sit.

"Watch out, Dad. He wants somethin'," Antoine walked in and said, rubbing his eyes.

"I just want to show you how much you're appreciated," I added, making a fist at my annoying brother.

"It's not like you did anything special to make them. You just popped the waffles into the toaster," Antoine said, trying to be a smarty and showing me two fists back.

I shot back at him, "So! You didn't pop any waffles in the toaster for Dad. And if you wanna eat some, the box is in the freezer. You can pop some in for yourself."

"Boys, calm down. I don't want you taking any of this hostility to camp. I'm serious about this."

Antoine said, "I'm just sayin', Dad. He's always gettin' under my skin."

"I'm not doing anything to Antoine, Dad. I'm trying to do something good because I want to, and he's picking on me. He gets away with everything."

I was so mad. I put Dad's plate on the table and went up to my room. A few minutes later, I was getting dressed when Dad called me back to eat breakfast. I was super upset because my waffles had gotten cold. On top of that, I didn't want to sit across from Antoine, who was on me like a tick on a dog. Sadly for me, he was hard to get away from.

"Antoine, go and get dressed," Dad told him. Then he told me, "Son, it's my job to parent both of you guys. You may not like my tactics, but just because I didn't reprimand your brother doesn't mean I don't care. I've always told you that you can talk to me. So don't ever storm off from me like a two-year-old who can't have his way."

"You don't even wanna hear what I have to say."

"Don't think that and don't tell me what I'm not going to do, young man. Now, get your attitude together and finish eating so we can go."

Minutes later, we were off to camp. As we rode along in the car, there was nothing but silence. I kept looking out the window, thinking about how upset I was. As far as I was concerned, I didn't have anything more to say to Dad or Antoine.

When we arrived at the park, I got the biggest curve ball of all. What happened at breakfast was nothing compared to what happened next. In my wildest dreams, I never thought that my brother would become friends with a kid who gives me so much trouble.

As soon as we got to the camp, Antoine said good-bye to Dad and jumped out of the car. He jogged straight over in Tyrod's direction, and the two of them hung out all morning. I couldn't believe it. They were acting like they'd been friends forever.

At lunchtime, Jelani was sitting across from me at the picnic table. We couldn't even eat in peace with Tyrod and Antoine laughing so hard.

"Is it really that funny?" Jelani asked. I shook my head, feeling completely fed up with them both.

"Dude, you're cool," Tyrod said to Antoine in a loud voice.

I guess it should be no surprise that they were really getting along. They were so much alike. Tyrod wanted to talk loud and that made Antoine talk louder. They tried to outdo each other by seeing who could hit the ball farther. The competition kept heating up, and neither of them would give up.

Then it suddenly came to me. The thing they had in common was trying to get under my skin. As long as they could beat me at everything, both of them were happy. I had to stop letting them see me sweat.

When I went to the water fountain, Tyrod came over to

me. As I bent down to drink, he said, "I don't understand why you're not like your brother. But that's okay. We're gonna show you how to get things done."

Later on in the boy's washroom, Antoine said, "You really don't think Tyrod is cool, do you? But you're wrong."

"I never even talked to you about Tyrod before, so what are you talking about?"

"Yes, you did. That time when you went to Dad's office because of him."

"I went to Dad's office more than once because of him."

"Man. I'm just teasing you. You don't know how to take a joke. I overheard you and Dad talking about him. Don't worry, Tyrod and I are gonna ease up on you."

Now wasn't the moment to bring up the time when he and our cousin Lil' Pete ganged up on me. Back then, Antoine told Dad that he was going to be good. So why hadn't he squashed all that?

I walked away and just prayed, *"Lord, I don't think Tyrod and Antoine need to be friends. Why did we have to come to this camp? I don't want to see them laughing and playing all the time. I'm trying to be the bigger person, but they're making me feel small. How am I supposed to put up with their constant teasing? Help!"*

When I was waiting on Dad to pick us up, Coach Riley came over to the bench where I was sitting. "Young man," he said to me. "You know this camp is about baseball, but it's also about helping you boys grow up. I've been watching you. You can't always avoid your brother and your friend. You guys need to work together."

"Sir, Antoine is my brother, but Tyrod is not my friend. And when they act out, I don't want to be around either of them."

"You're letting them get under your skin. You're letting them take too much control over you." He was telling me something that I was already figuring out for myself, but I found myself saying, "No disrespect, sir, but I don't even wanna do this camp. I'd rather not be around some of these people."

"Well, your brother lives with you, and doesn't that Tyrod boy go to your school?" He was right, but I didn't answer.

"All I'm saying is you're always going to have to deal with people who give you a hard time for no reason. Just hold on tight. Don't let people get the best of you. In this life, you've got to keep going until the end. You can't quit."

Letter to Mom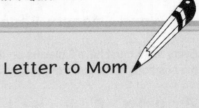

Dear Mom,

Once again I can't seem to get away from that troublemaker, Tyrod. Can you believe he is in the same baseball camp with me? In a strange way, I laughed when I found out. I think it will do him some good because the coach won't put up with his tricks. Tyrod had better watch himself.

To make things worse, Antoine and Tyrod have become good friends. They both like to get under my skin, and basically the coach told me not to let them see me sweat. I'm trying to get over my bad feelings because Dad wants me to give my all.

But, Mom, my ambition is not to become a good baseball player. The strong tactics the coach uses to motivate us makes me not want to play even more. I hope you understand because I'm like you, Mom. Neither one of us likes baseball.

Your son,
Mad Alec

Word Search: Baseball Positions

Every team must have 9 players on the field at all times. Some of the positions in the game of baseball are hidden in the puzzle.

```
P  O  W  E  R  H  I  T  T  E  R  U
I  N  A  M  E  S  A  B  N  Q  E  Y
N  C  N  C  D  B  R  E  T  I  H  G
C  N  R  A  L  W  Z  P  P  A  C  H
H  N  R  T  E  C  M  O  X  X  T  J
H  T  T  C  I  U  T  M  J  R  I  X
I  W  L  H  F  S  Z  O  O  W  P  Q
T  C  N  E  T  M  N  H  N  V  V  Z
T  G  Q  R  U  R  V  P  A  H  R  G
E  U  O  A  O  S  O  T  W  J  N  Q
R  H  D  W  E  D  L  U  F  B  X  B
S  S  W  O  V  I  P  E  N  M  O  Z
```

BASEMAN   CATCHER   OUTFIELDER
PINCHHITTER   PITCHER   POWERHITTER
(Pinch Hitter)   (Power Hitter)

SHORTSTOP

Trusting
God

3

"Why is hitting a baseball not easy for me? I don't like this sport!" I shouted, as I held the bat and hit the plate.

Coach said to me, "Son, you can't be hard on the equipment like that. Don't get frustrated. Learning the game of baseball and being successful at it takes work and practice."

I wanted to say, *I'm not your son. I don't like baseball, and I don't want to be here. I'm never going to be good at this, so I don't even care if the bat breaks.* But, of course, I said nothing because I'm supposed to be respectful of adults.

Then Tyrod stepped up behind me and said, "Move to the side. Let a pro do this. Give me that bat and get off the plate."

I wanted to not only drop the bat on the ground, but I also wanted to tell him to pick it up for himself. To make matters worse, on Tyrod's first swing he got a hit.

Antoine went behind him, and he wasn't much better than me. Watching him make a second strike made me think maybe the two of us should still try and talk our dad into letting us out of this baseball camp. Then, all of a sudden, the third pitch came and my brother somehow got into another zone. The ball hit the steel bat and went hurling high into the air. It went farther than any of the players out in the field could get to it.

My brother screamed out, "Yes!" He dropped the bat and threw both of his arms up in the air. "Who's the man?!" he shouted.

You would have thought he played in the major leagues because all of the kids in the camp went wild. Well, everybody except me. It wasn't that I wasn't happy for him. Antoine just proved that he was in a different league than me—and I didn't like that.

Even though he was better than me in basketball, I had skills too. Some days when I caught him off his game I could beat him. But baseball is a new sport for us. And if he could hit the ball out of the park and I couldn't hit it at all, that just didn't feel good to me.

I was glad when the end of the day came because I couldn't take any more embarrassment. At least, that was until Coach Riley called us all together in the center of the field and announced, "We've got an exhibition game coming up next week, and I want to do some extra practice with the following players."

Out of twenty kids, he named almost everyone. I was

one of the six that could go home.

Coach said, "I've already sent a text message to the parents of the fourteen that I want to stay. For the rest of you, don't be concerned. Everybody will have a chance to get good at baseball, it just takes work."

When Dad came to pick me up, I couldn't wait to get in the car.

"We aren't going to stay here and watch Antoine practice, are we? Please, Dad, I've been here all day."

"No, he's going to be here another couple of hours. I'll come back and get him. How about just you and I go and do something fun. What do you want to do? You hungry?"

Feeling like the day might finally be looking up, I said, "I'm always hungry."

"That's my boy, let's beef you up."

"I know, Dad, it's the eyeball test," I said, before he could say anything else.

He smiled and said, "That's right! You've got to have what?"

"Height, weight, and length," I recited.

"Exactly! So put on that weight. Let's go and get the works: a triple burger, some fries, and a shake."

When hearing that didn't really cheer me up, Dad asked, "Why are you looking so sad? It's not 'cause Coach didn't ask you to stay after for extra practice, is it?"

"Can I be honest, sir?" I asked, taking a deep breath.

"Alec, you can always talk to me. Of course, I want you to tell me the truth."

"I don't like the game of baseball. You know basketball is for me, Dad. I just want to have the ball in my hand, run with it, and try to dunk it. I don't want to have to hit a ball that can come at me in different ways—curve, fast, slow. It's just not me, Dad. Besides, I got all As on my report card. I shouldn't have to do a sport that I don't want to do."

"Coach says you have a lot of potential, Alec."

"Coach is just telling you that because he knows that every day at practice I'm frustrated and don't want to be there."

"Is it because your brother is doing well and you're struggling? You know, you could grow to like it, if you just give it time."

"I'm not Antoine, Dad. Yes, he picked up on baseball pretty good. He likes it now, and I don't. I just don't understand why you're forcing me to keep playing."

"I'm not taking you every morning with your hands tied behind your back."

"Yeah, but you're not letting me stay at home either. Come on, Dad, you know what I'm saying."

"I hear you, son, but I know you too. You like to be successful at things. Baseball is giving you a hard time. And, instead of embracing the challenge and figuring out what you need to do to get better at it, you just want to give up. I want you to stay because the lesson that you need to learn is inside you. I know you can learn to tough things out. If you hang in there now, it'll make you better in life."

"I understand what you mean, Dad, it's just that I don't like baseball."

"Think of it like a hard math problem you might face next year. You have to pass math on the CRCT, and it's going to get tougher. But just because you don't get it right away, are you going to quit? Are you going to drop it and go on to something else? Son, I'm trying to help you understand, if you quit without mastering the part that you didn't get, it's not going to help you in the end."

"That's academics, Dad. I have to do that."

"There's something inside of us all that makes us keep pushing forward. Otherwise, we'll just quit trying. Once you give up, then you're going to quit more times than you know. You're going to poke your lips out and get frustrated every time something gets hard. Alec, I'm telling you, going to summer camp is not about whether or not you like baseball. It's about finding something that doesn't come so easy to you and mastering it because you're determined not to give up until you do."

We pulled up to the restaurant, and I was still in a sad mood. I honestly wasn't feeling any better. Usually, when we eat out, all I think about is how much I'm going to eat. But this time I was thinking about what Dad said, not about how much I would enjoy the food. This time I was thinking about the fact that he was right.

Baseball definitely didn't come easy to me. And the strange thing about it was, I said I didn't like it before I started playing. For the past two weeks, I hadn't given much effort. Maybe if I tried harder, I could find success in something that wasn't easy. Just maybe.

● ● ●

"Mom! I just can't believe you're here!" I said, as I jumped out of bed and hugged my mom real tight. She was waking me up on the morning of my brother's thirteenth birthday party.

"Alec, your mama ain't gon' be able to breathe," Grandma said with a big smile, when she saw I wasn't going to let my mom go.

"Yeah! Get off Mom. She's here for *my* birthday!" Antoine said, shoving me over. He had followed Mom and Grandma into my room.

"Antoine, be nice," Mom said before reaching out to hold me again.

"Alec, you can hug me anytime, honey," she looked down at me and said with a smile.

At that moment, Mom was the most beautiful lady I've ever seen. Not because she's a star and not because she's my mom, but because she has such a big heart. My mother wants everyone in the world to get along. She really wants everyone to be as happy as she is. I really can't remember seeing her this lovely in a long time.

Looking up at her pretty face, I couldn't help but smile back at her. "What are you smiling at, babe?" she asked, as she took me by my hand. Her touch felt so good, as she rubbed my back.

"I'm just happy that you're happy. I'm even happier that you're here. I just love you, Mom, that's all."

A little while later, Dad, Grandma, and Antoine loaded up the car and headed over to the clubhouse. Antoine was having a pool party for his birthday and he couldn't wait. I stayed behind with Mom to help finish decorating the birthday cake. But I really just wanted to be alone with her. Any one-on-one time I could have with her, I wanted to soak up like a sponge.

"Alec, I've been reading your letters, but I'm here now. Is there anything you want to talk to me about specifically? Anything that's been going on that you want to share with me? Is everything okay with you?"

After I took a minute to think, I opened up like a flood-gate. "Antoine gives me a hard time. Dad's makin' me play baseball and I don't want to play. The guy from my class who pushed all of my buttons is at camp too, so I'm still stuck with being around him. I get teased a lot because Dad's an administrator at my school. I miss my mom every day. I don't know. I guess other than dealing with all of that, I'm okay."

Seeing her begin to get teary made me start praying, *"Lord, I'm sorry. I didn't mean to hurt my mom's feelings. I don't know what to say. I'm glad she's here. I'm just trying to be honest."*

"I'm so sorry, Mom," I said, when I saw a tear fall.

"You don't have to worry about me. I'm okay." She reached over and hugged me tight.

"I know things have been a little difficult around here, even though your grandmother has helped out in every way she can. Your dad's been doing the best he can. And your brother is dealing with all this too. My being away so long may not be the best for us. That's why I can't continue on the show. I'm going to quit."

I knew she wasn't just telling me something that I wanted to hear. Although she must have thought about it a lot, the fact that she had decided to quit was going to be a very big sacrifice for her.

At the same time, it was one she was willing to make for us, or maybe just for me. Dad and Antoine had given her space and Grandma understood that Mom needed to do something big for herself. That's why my grandmother was willing to help us out. She wanted Mom to become the best mom that she could be for Antoine and me.

All of that made me think about what Mom needed more than about what I wanted. I love her and want her to be happy, so I said, "Mom, you can't quit. We're all proud that you're on TV. It's your dream. Please don't quit."

Tears rolled down her face, and she hugged me again. It was a special moment . . . one that I'd remember when she was far away. She did love her little boy and was willing to give up her big shot at being famous. But I love her too, and I just couldn't let her do it. She was supposed to be leaving to go back to California tomorrow, and here she was talking about not returning. I had to make sure she went.

"My youngest son is growing up."

"Well, like Dad said, I've got to start facing tough things and pushing my way through them."

"We'd better get going. We can't have a party without the birthday cake," she said, as she wiped her eyes. I was glad to see her sad face turn happy again.

When we got to the pool, all of the joy I was feeling quickly turned to shock. The first person I saw was Tyrod. I was carrying the cake and almost dropped it. I mean, it wasn't my party or anything but Antoine didn't even tell me that he was inviting Tyrod. It's not that he had to, but I sure didn't like the smug look on Tyrod's face. It was as if he knew that Antoine didn't tell me. When he opened his mouth to speak, in a flash I was reminded why we weren't friends.

"What's up, dude? You surprised to see me at your brother's party? What can I say? Your brother's cool and you're not. Besides, it's not a party until Tyrod shows up. Hey, you still lickin' your wounds from not being able to hit the little baseball, little boy?" Tyrod said, once again getting under my skin.

As soon as he saw Mom whip around the corner, he completely changed. "Hello, ma'am! You must be Antoine's mom. Can I help you carry that? Those bags look mighty heavy."

Before Mom could say anything, Tyrod was taking the load out of her hands.

"What a gentleman you are! Thank you very much. I

hope my boys are this helpful to adults," Mom gushed.

"Antoine is very helpful and at camp he's always there for the coach. But I can't say the same about Alec," Tyrod replied.

"What? Alec, you don't help out?" My mother frowned at me, believing Tyrod's phony story.

Slowly and angrily, I gritted my teeth and said, "Mom, this is TYROD."

She looked at me and raised her eyebrows. I gave her a quick nod. She got it. The meanest boy from my class was giving her a false image of himself.

"I didn't know Antoine invited him to the party. We're gonna have so much fun," I added sarcastically.

As Tyrod started toward the table with Mom's bags, he said, "I can tell he doesn't like me very much, Mrs. London. I want to try and be his friend, but he just won't give me the time of day."

I couldn't believe the garbage he was feeding my mother. All I could do was shake my head. Then Mom said, "You know what . . . Tyrod, come on back. The two of you guys need to talk for a minute."

Glad that I had the big old cake in my hand, I looked at her and then motioned down at it. Mom said, "Okay, okay, come on and put the cake down, Alec. But before this day is over, I want you two to talk."

"You know I don't wanna talk to you or be your friend, right?" Tyrod whispered, as we walked behind her.

All I said was, "Ditto." Somehow I could tell that he

didn't like the fact that I didn't care.

But Tyrod didn't know what really got to me was the fact that Antoine thought he was super cool. For the rest of the day, when Antoine needed help passing something out, he called on Tyrod. When he wanted to race someone in the water, he called for Tyrod. When he wanted to divide up into swim teams, the first person he had on his team was Tyrod.

I didn't like watching Antoine bond with Tyrod—as if he had a new little brother all of a sudden. The only thing that made me keep my cool was the fact that it wasn't my birthday. It was Antoine's day, and if Tyrod could make Antoine happy by being his buddy, then it wasn't for me to poke my lips out about it.

I just went along with it, even though I felt like an outsider at my own brother's birthday party. I couldn't tell my parents about it because they were enjoying each other and I certainly liked seeing them have fun together.

My grandmother was busy being a lifeguard so I couldn't go to her either. She couldn't swim a lick but she sure didn't mind yelling at the kids to make sure they stayed safely away from the water when they weren't in it. So, I just had to deal with it on my own. I admit that seeing Tyrod and Antoine laughing every five seconds wasn't easy.

The very next day, we all said our good-byes and Dad took Mom to the airport. This time, I smiled and kissed her on the cheek before she left. After she and I had our talk, I was okay with her leaving. The glowing smile she gave me back said it all for me. Mom and I were cool with each other.

● ● ●

"Oh, my goodness! No! No!" Grandma shouted and dropped the phone.

The news she just heard seemed really hard to take because she broke down, clutched her stomach, and started sobbing. Dad picked up the phone and spoke to whoever was on the other end. Antoine was outside and came rushing in when he heard Grandma's cries.

"What's wrong? What's wrong?" he asked me.

I pointed to Grandma. Seeing her so upset made me worry, but I didn't know what to do. I tried to help her up, but she tugged away as if the spot I touched was causing her pain. I didn't take it personally because I knew something was very wrong.

After Dad hung up the phone, he said, "Come on, Mom. Let's go to the hospital. You have to stay positive. You have to have faith. Dot's going to be okay."

"What's wrong with Aunt Dot?" Antoine asked, his voice trembling.

He spoke for me at that moment. We hadn't known Aunt Dot very well until this year. Since Grandma's been staying at our house, Aunt Dot has been around a lot. That gave me a chance to get to know her better. She's a sweet lady. I just hope she'll be okay.

Dad came over to me and Antoine and touched us both

firmly on the shoulders. "Boys, I'm going to need you to keep it together," he told us.

"What's wrong with Aunt Dot?" This time I asked.

"She fell down the stairs and there is some severe bleeding going on. She's in the hospital and unconscious right now. I'm going to take your grandmother to the hospital. I'll be back as soon as I can. Just stay here and pray."

"Yes, sir," we both said at the same time.

"Boys, y'all pray for my sister now, please!" Grandma said, as she walked out of the house with Dad.

"I don't know how to pray," Antoine turned to me and said. "You do it!"

"We can pray together."

"Okay. Just say whatever. I'm with you."

I reached my hand out. My brother looked at me like I had lost my mind. But if we were gonna do this, we had to mean it. We both were shaking, but we had to be together in our prayer.

Once he gave me his hand, I said, "Let's bow our heads."

I didn't really know if I was saying the right thing. I had never prayed with Antoine before, but I talk to the Lord a lot. I was just going to do it the same way now.

So I began to pray, *"Lord, Antoine and I are coming to You, asking You to help Aunt Dot. Something serious is going on with her and she's in the hospital. We ask You right now to take care of her, heal her, and make everything okay with her. We also pray for our Grandma, that she would be calm. She loves You so much, Lord. I pray that she won't be worried but that she can be at peace and be there for her sister. We also pray for Lil' Pete. In Jesus' name. Amen."*

"Why did you pray for him?" Antoine asked me, as he let go of my hand. I could see him rolling his eyes.

"I don't know. I just feel like we would need prayer if it was our grandmother. We already feel sad, and she's our great aunt. Remember how we felt when Grandma went to the hospital? I mean, imagine how Lil' Pete must be feeling right now. Aunt Dot is all he's got. It doesn't seem bad to pray for him, does it?"

Antoine shook his head. "It's just weird, I guess. The way he treated you and now you're prayin' for him."

"It's called grace. It comes from God. I know that I don't deserve a whole lot of things. I believe God sent His Son to die on the cross for me so I could be forgiven. Now He wants me to forgive others."

"Well, it ain't that easy for me. I ain't wishin' nothin' bad on Lil' Pete or anything, but he just thinks he's all that. If I don't do what he says, then I'm not cool. He was so rough with you. I can't believe you forgive him."

"I forgive him, but I haven't forgotten. I'm workin' on that. But for real, he's goin' through a lot right now, and I know God can make it better for him."

Antoine didn't respond. I could tell he was thinking about what I said even though he was gritting his teeth. I wanted to tell him that he needed to open his heart to God, but I didn't press him.

About three hours later, I didn't have to imagine how Lil' Pete was doing because he came in the front door with my father. Grandma was staying at the hospital with her sister and insisted that he stay with us. Lil' Pete had nowhere else to go. I was okay with it, but Antoine was pacing back and forth in his room.

"Anywhere but here . . . I can't believe that he had to come here. Doesn't anybody else care about him? I don't want him here, and I'm going to go and tell Dad."

I tried to stop him before he could get close to Dad. It was already a terrible situation. He didn't need to add to it by not making our home a friendly place for Lil' Pete.

Before he knew what was happening, Antoine was stopped dead in his tracks when he walked into Dad's office. There was Lil' Pete, in tears, in Dad's arms.

This wasn't fake; it wasn't made up. He wasn't trying to be funny. He was hurting, and it was very hard for both of us to watch. Antoine grabbed my arm and squeezed it kind of hard. I thought he was going to choke up when he saw Lil' Pete that way.

I just prayed again, but silently this time. *"Lord, I don't know what's going on with Aunt Dot, but by the way Lil' Pete is acting upset, I hope the worst hasn't happened. And I know it's not supposed to be so bad when we die 'cause when we accept You, we'll be in heaven. But sometimes we just want people around longer to tell them how much we care. We need to tell them we're sorry and how much we love them. Some part of me knows that Lil' Pete needs to tell his grandma that he's sorry, but I'm not judging. I love You, Lord, and I ask that You give me and Antoine whatever we need to help him through this."*

● ● ●

Over the next week, Dad spent a lot of time with Lil' Pete. Aunt Dot was still in intensive care, and all they were telling us was that it was a touch-and-go situation. We could only hope for the best and leave it in God's hands. It was very hard, but we were all trusting God.

Letter to Mom

Dear Mom,

We are facing a serious situation with Aunt Dot. She's in the hospital and unconscious. I'm very concerned for her health, and I'm praying that she'll recover and get well. I believe the Lord hears our prayers.

You talk about a bunch of messy situations. We have our fair share of them. Now you want to sacrifice your career to come home to us. Like I said to you before you left, I can't let you do that. Even though you're miles away, we're united and our prayers will make everything okay.

> Your son,
> Faithful Alec

Word Search: Baseball Fouls

You must follow the important rules of baseball if you don't want to get your team in trouble. Listed below are some of the most frequent fouls incurred when playing the game of baseball. Find them in the puzzle.

```
P  L  G  J  U  A  Q  W  J  G  V  J
V  G  B  C  O  P  U  R  R  B  S  M
K  L  W  D  E  G  O  O  E  A  A  L
L  E  B  W  H  W  U  R  N  U  V  G
O  L  E  L  A  N  I  R  U  L  Y  Y
N  M  A  I  D  L  O  E  S  G  F  M
A  Q  N  B  A  L  K  M  C  K  N  V
F  N  A  X  L  I  U  E  O  K  P  D
R  L  I  P  R  U  G  I  P  H  A  N
L  P  I  T  C  H  O  U  T  Y  T  E
T  J  S  J  V  N  W  F  N  T  U  G
L  X  K  O  Y  I  Z  I  B  G  V  L
```

BALK	ERROR	FOULBALL	GROUNDBALL
		(Foul Ball)	(Ground Ball)
	PITCHOUT	STRIKE	WALK

Fair Chance

4

"**No, Alec!** I don't wanna play with Lil' Pete. Yeah, he's stayin' in our house, and he's got Dad all wrapped around his finger. But he's not a cool dude. I don't even wanna see his face—so don't ask me again!" Antoine snapped at me.

A part of me wanted to yell out, *Fine then! Don't play with Lil' Pete!* Another part of me just wanted to agree and say, *Cool, Antoine. I understand.* So I was torn and didn't know what to do. I didn't even know what was right. I mean, Lil' Pete had been bad before, but he was doing better.

Aunt Dot was still very ill and in the hospital. At the least, we could accept him because of her. I'm sure she wouldn't want us acting this way.

That made me pray, *"Lord, I need You to help me. Teach me what I should do. I used to be sort of jealous of Antoine and Lil' Pete's relationship. They used to leave me out, and now they're not even speaking to each other. Antoine is really mad and doesn't want to forgive Lil' Pete. But I'm actually feeling sorry for him. He's worried about his grand-mother's health. Now we're living under the same roof. Help us come together and lean on each other. As strange as it seems, I'm the youngest, and right now I'm acting like the oldest."*

As soon as I got up off my knees, Antoine came over to me and said, "I know you said you wanna play with Lil' Pete. But I've got reasons why I don't."

"Okay, so why are you standing at my door? Because I could go and play with him without you, and you'd be watching from the window, wanting to come out."

"Whatever. No, I won't."

Trying another angle, I said, "Well, what if I go out there to play with him and he gets rough with me and I don't have my big brother to take up for me?"

Antoine paused for a second and said, "Yeah, you're right. I should go out there with you guys. He's been acting all chummy around our dad and then acting different when it's just us two. Lil' Pete knows what he's doing when he gives me the silent treatment. I don't trust him."

"Antoine, just talk to him."

"Huh, I already told you I'm not tryin' to be his buddy."

A few minutes later, we headed downstairs to find Lil' Pete. He was stretched out on the sofa in the family room.

"I'm watchin' somethin' on this TV," he said to the two of us before we said anything to him, "so don't touch the remote."

"See?" Antoine said to me and crossed his arms. He was ready to give up and walk away.

I grabbed him by the back of his shirt and said, "No, you're not going anywhere. This doesn't have to be a competition between the three of us about who's the biggest and the baddest. Just chill."

"Y'all don't even wanna hang out with me, so what are you doin' down here anyway? If I can't hang with your dad, then I'm good by myself," said Lil' Pete.

"I'm sorry about that," I said to Lil' Pete.

"Sorry? I'm not sorry," Antoine added. "You didn't even ask to play with us. You just went straight to our dad with your sob story . . . like you're the only one who has stuff goin' on. We've got stuff goin' on too. Besides, you never even apologized to my brother for bullying him. Why should we like you?"

Lil' Pete stood up and walked up close to Antoine's face. I was hoping the two of them weren't going to fight. Then, Lil' Pete surprised me when he opened his mouth.

"You're right. I'm sorry, Antoine." Then he turned to me and said, "I'm sorry, Lil Man. I've got a problem with opening up to people and saying how I feel."

"Thanks, man, I accept your apology. But, you got to try sometime and give a little effort. It might come easier than you think to be cool with people," I said to him.

Lil' Pete put his hand on his head. "Y'all don't understand. Y'all have it so good and easy."

Antoine said, "Easy? Where have you been, man? Our

mom is way across the country, out in California!"

"Yeah, but all y'all have been talkin' about is how your family is goin' out there for a month. My grandmother's in the hospital, fighting for her life. If she leaves, who's gonna take me in? Y'all don't want me here. I wish your dad was my dad. He's cool. My dad didn't even want me!" Lil' Pete covered his face as though he was about to cry.

"You don't know that," I said. It just felt like the right thing to say. I couldn't imagine what he must be feeling to never have his dad in his life. Then he started telling us about how he had to grow up without his father. I could hear in his voice that he wanted his dad to do better so they could be together.

Lil' Pete turned his back to us, walked over to the window, and looked out. "My dad never took me outside to throw a baseball with me. He's never cooked a meal for me. He doesn't care about my grades. I have no father."

"What about your mom?" I asked, until Antoine quickly put his hands over my mouth. I didn't know what was wrong. Antoine and Lil' Pete used to talk, but I never knew his story.

"It's okay, man," Lil' Pete said to Antoine. "My mom died. I was little, like three." He paused and took a deep breath. "Even though she's not here with me, I believe she's in a better place. My dad is alive, but he doesn't even show his face. He never even calls. It's different for you guys. Your mom is away, but at least she's still a part of your family. She calls all the time and even visits sometimes. Y'all have a cool relationship. I guess I act out and cut up because deep down inside I'm broken worse than an egg that got cracked open and scrambled."

Antoine went over to him and said, "I just kept thinking about myself, you know? I was so worried about you moving in on my family that I didn't even think about your problems. Alec is right. We're family. Let's stop fightin' against each other. We've all got issues. Maybe we can be there for each other and make life a little easier."

Seeing the two of them hug and forgive each other was awesome. I looked out the window and whispered, "Thank You, God." We couldn't solve Lil' Pete's problems, and he couldn't solve ours. But at least we could have each others' backs. And that was worth so much more.

● ● ●

"Come on, guys. The way you're warming up with such poor effort isn't going to help you or your team."

I wanted to tell Coach Riley that I couldn't care less about giving my all for baseball. This was not my sport. Even though I wasn't good at it and he knew it, he was putting every player into the rotation.

Then Coach said in a serious voice, "If you give a little effort now and you're not warmed up, not focused, and not listening to my coaching, how do you think you'll be when it's game time? I'll tell you how—unprepared. Young men, it's time to get it to together."

"I'm all about game time, Coach," Tyrod spoke up.

"Me and my man here, Antoine, we're superstars. We're all that counts."

"I know that's your brother and all," Jelani said in my ear. "But I'm gettin' tired of them thinkin' they're the boss just because they can hit a couple of long balls."

Before the game started, I watched the other team jog onto the field with energy, quickly make two lines, and do strong jumping jacks to warm up.

Coach Riley noticed it too. He was more than a little upset that we didn't have the same fire. When the game started, no one was really into it. Nobody wanted to pitch. Nobody was trying to catch to their best ability. From an outsider, we were just going through the motions, and our head wasn't in the game.

We have some great players on our team, but we weren't working together. When the umpire blew the whistle to play, we froze. We didn't put much effort into winning the game. Our team got tired quickly. Even when people hit, they didn't match the determination of the other team, and we struck out.

When it was time for the other team to bat, not only could they hit hard—they were fast. It was so plain to me that they played like a team who came to win. One person was willing to get himself out by playing in between bases so that our team would work hard to get one person out. What a great strategy. They got two runs that way.

The only thing the players on our team seemed to care about was getting attention for themselves. It was no surprise that our attitude cost us the game.

When we left the ballpark, there was nothing but silence. When our bus pulled up in front of the restaurant, Coach stood up, and we all stood up with him.

"Sit down," he said. "What I saw today really bothered me. It showed that you put so little in and that's why you got little results. Besides, I thought you all would have cared more about the team than yourselves. You've got to know that you have to change your selfish attitude into a positive one if you want to win. Now I see what you all are excited about. You can't wait to get off of this bus to eat a burger. You need to have that kind of fire in everything you do."

"We can't win every game, Coach," Tyrod said with a loud grunt.

"That's not my point, young man. It's not about winning or losing, it's about how you play the game. You have to play with the right attitude. It puts you in the right frame of mind to win. That goes for anything in life—if you want to win, you've got to give it all you've got."

"And speak for yourself, Tyrod," Antoine spoke up and said, being the brother I knew who always speaks his mind. "I don't like losing."

I was kind of proud that he stood up to Tyrod and showed how he felt. Tyrod quickly changed his tune like somebody changing the channel on a TV. He knew he wanted to keep my brother's friendship. I just shook my head.

"Yeah. I mean, I like winning too, Coach, and I know we all can do better."

"Well, we've got one more game tomorrow. If you really want to prove yourselves as a team to me, then don't talk about it. Be about it."

Later that night, Antoine came in my room. "You know, you really can play baseball. Right?"

I was shocked and surprised at his statement. Was my big brother really trying to encourage me?

Antoine explained what he meant. "I'm talking about when you're standing at bat. If you slide up a few more inches and tilt your head like you know what you're doing, you could really knock that ball out of the park."

"No, you're a way better athlete than me," I said.

"Alec, man, if you really put your mind to it, you'll be unstoppable."

"Really? You think so?"

He nodded. "I didn't like losing today. That loss could have been prevented. Tomorrow when we go against our last team, I'm going to step up as captain. We need to go out there strong. We may not ever play baseball again, but at least we'll give it everything we've got. Let's not go out like wimps. You down?"

"Yeah, man." And I meant it.

The next morning, we arrived at the park all fired up. Antoine and I kept our same enthusiasm from our talk the night before and it spread to the other players. The guys caught wind of it, and everybody was hyped and ready to go. Not only did we have a lot of fun because we gave it our all, but we beat the other team. It was a close game, but we pulled it out by one run. We actually tried and succeeded!

Coach had taught us something valuable and we learned the lesson of whatever you put in, that's what you get out. We were actually winners. I'd never forget what Dad taught me too. He told me whether I liked something or not, I always needed to do my best. Besides that, I remembered Antoine's advice about having confidence in myself. And, sure enough, I was the one who hit the winning home run. From now on, I'm not going to give a little. I'm going to give my all.

● ● ●

"Mom! I didn't know you were coming here," I yelled out, as I sprang into her arms. I was really surprised and glad to see her.

In fact, everything was looking good. Aunt Dot was getting out of the hospital. My grandma and Lil' Pete were going to stay with her and look after her. We were sad that Lil' Pete was leaving us now that Antoine and I both bonded with him. However, now it was time for us to get our family back together and on track.

"I love you, Alec. Oh, I missed you so much! I'm so excited that we all get to spend the Fourth of July holiday together. We're going to have a lot of fun together this month!"

When I pulled back from hugging my mom, I noticed

Lil' Pete was watching us from the dining room. I didn't say anything to him. Mom must have seen him too because she pulled away from me.

"Sweetie, I need to talk to your dad in private really quick. I'll see you in a second, okay?"

I was so glad to see my mother and I never wanted to let go of her. It's a good thing that I wanted to talk to Lil' Pete. Or I would have acted like a big baby and hung on to my mom's leg or something. Instead, I did the mature thing and walked over to my cousin.

"You okay?" I asked Lil' Pete.

He just looked away. It was hard for me to see my big, strong cousin struggle to keep his emotions together. He was hurting on the inside.

"I'm cool. You know, over the last couple of weeks I've been watchin' you prayin', readin' the Bible, and gettin' along with people."

"You can pray too, Lil' Pete."

"I don't even know if I believe in God. It's hard to think that God would allow a boy not to have a mom or dad. I can understand my mom bein' in heaven, but for Him to give me a dad who doesn't care . . . that's hard to get. I don't remember much about my mom, but it's been tough with her not here, especially since my dad's not with me. That's not so easy to take."

"You're tough. I wish I was as strong as you," I said, trying to keep him uplifted.

"Being strong doesn't make it better. It can make you

so mean on the inside that you don't have it in your heart to forgive," Lil' Pete said before he paused. Then he surprised me and said, "But when I see God in you, I want that."

"Come on, Lil' Pete. Let's go," Grandma called out.

As we said good-bye to Lil' Pete and kissed Grandma, a part of me knew he wanted to go with us to California, but I also knew he wanted to make sure his grandmother was okay. Plus, our family needed some alone time. Lil' Pete gave me a fist bump, and I told him to keep his head up.

Antoine had taken some stuff out to the cab for Grandma. When he came back in the house, he said, "You know somethin' is up with our folks?"

Not having a clue, I said, "What do you mean?"

"I'm sayin' Mom and Dad have been weird since Mom got here."

"Actually, she left me and said she needed to go and talk to Dad. I didn't even know that she was comin' here. I thought we were gonna meet her in L.A."

"Yeah, well, there's a reason she came back. They've been locked in their room for a while now. I don't know what's goin' on. You don't think they're breakin' up, do you?" Antoine asked. I could see the worry on his face, like a kid who's scared to see his grade after taking a hard test.

"No. Are you crazy? The way he's been texting her and calling her. He misses her. I know their relationship is good."

"It's still weird. What's goin' on then?"

"Nothing's wrong. I have faith that everything is okay. That's what you should have too, Antoine."

When my parents came out, they both looked like they had lost their best friend. Their faces looked tired. They looked like they had lost all hope.

Antoine jumped the gun and said, "Okay, tell us. What's wrong?"

"Andre, this is going to be hard. I can't tell them," Mom said.

"Tell us what? We can't go to California? We're gonna have to stay here? What kinda camp are you gonna put us in now, Dad?" Antoine said with attitude.

Dad said in his serious voice, "Watch your mouth, young man."

Antoine softened his tone, "I'm just sayin'. You promised us this trip."

Mom replied, "That's not it. You're going to California. Andre, tell them."

I looked over at Dad and asked, "What's wrong?"

I wanted to ask if they were breaking up, but I had just told Antoine to have faith. I couldn't lose the faith I had at this point. There was no way it could happen. My parents were going to be together forever.

"Boys, you're still going to California with your mom. It's just that I can't go. We can't go as a family."

"What do you mean, you can't go?" Antoine asked. "Grandma is fine. What's holdin' you back?"

I chimed in. "Yeah, Dad. We're all supposed to be there together."

"Boys, I have to stay back because of my job. Your Mom's here to fly back with you guys."

"Did you tell them you had a family vacation? July is supposed to be the month that you have off. I don't understand. Don't you care? You gotta go with us," I said, as tears started to roll down my face. I couldn't hold them back.

Dad just looked away. I wanted this for so long. This was our big chance to be a family. We had already worked it out so he could go. I didn't know anything about business or being an adult, but I knew we needed money to pay our bills. Both our parents were working. Mom was doing a TV show, and Dad had a full-time job as an assistant principal. Something wasn't adding up, and I was lost.

I couldn't understand. Didn't he care about being with his family? Why wasn't he explaining? Why wasn't he trying? Didn't he want us to be together? Why wasn't he giving his family a fair chance?

Letter to Mom

Dear Mom,

I know Antoine is the oldest, but he can be so childish. He doesn't know that how he acts sometimes is annoying. But, sometimes he surprises me when he tries to make things right.

It makes me happy when he shows me that he cares. He even told me that I could be good at baseball, a sport I'm not good at. So honestly, it seems our relationship is still strong. I was getting tired of his poor effort, but now I see he's trying. Cool, huh?

I don't get it. I'm sad that Dad's not coming with us to California. Now I know what adults mean when they say, "It's always something."

Your son,

Upset Alec

Word Search: MLB Teams

The ultimate level of playing baseball is the pros, also called Major League Baseball. Below are some of the top teams in MLB. See if you can find them all.

```
S  K  B  A  H  I  U  K  C  N  L  V
D  L  Y  Y  Y  Z  X  O  S  D  E  R
A  N  A  O  T  I  D  A  D  Y  M  Y
N  G  N  N  S  Z  A  E  H  Z  E  S
M  X  K  K  I  N  U  H  Z  P  P  S
G  S  E  G  C  D  A  A  U  I  H  K
U  X  E  Z  I  E  R  I  B  W  I  C
M  T  S  N  J  U  L  A  D  K  L  L
S  R  E  G  N  A  R  T  C  N  L  K
W  L  J  K  S  E  P  U  I  Q  I  W
K  M  W  V  N  P  D  Q  L  C  E  O
S  E  V  A  R  B  J  G  T  J  S  D
```

BRAVES	**CARDINALS**	**INDIANS**
PHILLIES	**RANGERS**	**RED SOX**
YANKEES		

Big Deal

5

"**What do you** mean, Dad's going to be the principal at my school?" I asked Mom when she, Antoine, and I were on the plane headed to California.

"It just became official. He got the job this morning. See, here's the text." She proudly handed me her phone.

I didn't really want to look at it. I just turned my head and shook it really hard. This couldn't be happening. No way could my father be the principal of my elementary school. Finally, I make it to the fifth grade, the oldest class in the building, and now he's gonna mess that up.

"It's not all about you, ya know," Antoine said, bumping me in the arm.

I didn't like sitting between him and Mom on the plane. It was a tight spot. I wanted to be by the window so I could look out at the sky and all the clouds. Or I wouldn't mind sitting in the aisle seat where I could have elbow room and get up anytime I wanted. But Mom had the aisle and Antoine was sitting by the window.

"I'm not talkin' to you," I said to Antoine.

"Okay, but you need to chill because Dad getting a promotion means buying more clothes, more video games, a nicer ride . . . you're trippin'."

I shouted back, "You're trippin'!"

My mother gave us the "calm down" look and said, "Both of you guys settle down. And, Antoine, just because your dad's making more money doesn't mean you need to have dollar signs spinning through your mind, thinking you can spend it all."

"Mom, I don't know what kind of debt we were in after he lost his job, but with you working and Dad getting a promotion, I can't help it if I'm excited. Now it can be like the old days. I still remember the way it used to be. It was fun being spoiled."

She shook her head. "And the one good thing about us going through hard times was that we couldn't give you boys everything you wanted. That's not how life works, Antoine."

Mom could handle Antoine, so I wasn't really listening. Even though the two of them were talking across me, I was so into the fact that Dad was going to be principal of my school next year, I didn't know what to do. It was bad enough with me getting teased when he was the assistant. Now that he'd be the head guy, I would never hear the end of it. I could already hear Tyrod saying, "The only reason the teachers are bein' nice to you is because you're the principal's son."

80

I didn't want to be picked on and have any special favors done for me. I didn't want my father to be the principal. So as hard as I could, I threw my head back and hit it against my seat. Mom grabbed my hand and squeezed it real tight. She wasn't saying anything to me, but I could tell she was trying to say, *It's going to be okay, honey, don't worry.*

Then Antoine tried to get under my skin when he leaned over and whispered in my ear. "You need your mommy to pet you. Aw! Ain't that sweet?"

When we touched down in Los Angeles, I still had my lips poked out. I didn't mean to be bummed out, but how could I be happy? Finding out that Dad was going to have the head job at my school was bad news for me.

Still, I had to smile a little seeing how happy Mom was. I could tell she really liked this big, sunny, west coast state.

My brother was like a kid in a toy store, "Wow, this airport is nice."

Mom touched my shoulder and said, "Are you okay, honey?"

I had to remember that this wasn't all about me. She seemed very excited to have us with her, and I didn't want to spoil it for her. I knew I needed to get my act together, so I said, "I'm okay."

Then she told me, "I know things aren't just the way you like them, but your dad and I are really trying."

"I know, Mom. It's just hard."

"I understand. I get that, son," she said. Somehow I got the feeling she really did.

"I missed out on some precious time with you over the last year. And I plan to make up for some of that lost time over the next few weeks."

I had to believe her too. As soon as we got off the plane and picked up our bags, a driver was waiting to take us on a tour. We drove from Malibu to see the beach, to Hollywood to see the stars. Though I had seen most of the sites the first time I was there, they were still the coolest things I've ever seen . . . a completely different world. Taking it all in again gave me an exciting feeling. It told me that I could keep on going, dreaming about what my life could be like. I was beginning to understand that I could become anything I wanted.

Mom's new place was larger. She lives in a two-bedroom condo, and the building looks like a hotel. There's an indoor swimming pool, an arcade room, and even a gym.

Antoine was so thrilled. He asked her, "What are we gonna do tomorrow? Can we please go to where the Lakers play?"

Before she could answer, her cell phone rang. When she answered it, the smile on her face turned to a frown. "Are you serious? No way! I thought we were good for now . . . well, okay then."

As soon as she hung up, my brother and I just stared at her, waiting to hear something. She sighed and said, "I'm sorry, boys, our plans are going to have to change. We have to reshoot a few scenes and they want us to do some promotion commercials."

"What?" I asked.

"We're still going to have our time, boys. Don't look so disappointed. I'll be shooting in the morning and I'll be done in the afternoon."

"That's good. We can sleep in."

"Um, no, son. I've enrolled you in an acting camp with a very special lady. I can't wait for you to meet her."

"I don't care how special the lady is! I don't wanna be an actor!" Antoine said, with his face turning to a frown.

"Ditto!" I said really loud.

Antoine started complaining big time. I was with him on this one. But I could tell we were making Mom feel bad.

Mom let out a groan and said, "Well, you're not going to like every decision that I make. I'm the adult, and I know what's best for you. How will you ever know if you like something or not until you try it? You're going to take the lessons, and you're going to have the right attitude doing it. Any problem with that?"

Neither of us said a word. But Mom had a message for us. She said, "Good. You're learning. Sometimes you're going to have to deal with things you disagree with. Just know that the people who get ahead in the world are the ones who don't get upset every time they hear news they don't like."

● ● ●

"So I wonder why your mom just dropped you off," the lady said to us when we arrived at the theater. In a weird way, she reminded me of Mom but was way older.

Wanting her to understand that my mother was busy, I tried to explain. "She was in a real big hurry, ma'am. She got a call and they moved up the time that she was supposed to be at work. She said you'd be expecting us. I'm sure if she knew it was a problem, she would've made the time to come in and speak."

"Look at you . . . taking up for your mom, Alec, huh?"

I nodded and said, "Yes, ma'am."

"I still don't understand what kind of mom would just drop her kids off without making sure they're in a safe environment."

It was Antoine's turn. "I don't understand what kind of teacher or adult would talk about someone's mom in front of her kids. My brother just told you she was busy. You need to take that up with her, not us. Do you want her number?"

The lady who was talking kind of mean to us looked my brother over and surprised me by saying, "I like you."

That made no sense to me. How could she like him? He was rude. My mom would ground him if she knew he sounded so rough.

"You tell it like it is. Give me a high five." She raised her hand high so that she could slap hands with Antoine.

"Antoine, you're being rude," I whispered.

"No, he's not being rude," she said to me. "He's not letting anybody push him around. Both of you young men have qualities I admire. Hmmm . . . interesting . . . very interesting. Well, quit staring at me! Get a move on in there!" she demanded, as she pointed to the auditorium.

It was a small theater, but it was very important looking. There were about one hundred seats and a nice stage with a red velvet curtain.

Walking toward the front, I noticed there were three other students. A girl who was taller than Antoine was chewing bubblegum on the stage. Once she was caught, the mean lady said, "Now you know that I don't tolerate any gum chewing on the stage. How can you say your lines properly if you're chewing gum? Take it out, and put it on your nose."

The tall girl said, "Huh? Ms. Ana that's not cool."

I'm glad the girl said her name because the lady hadn't even bothered to tell us, even though she knew our names.

"It will make you remember not to chew gum in my theater again. ON YOUR NOSE!" Ms. Ana said very loudly.

Now, of course, Antoine wanted to laugh. Ms. Ana glared at him and that made him hold it together.

Then there was a boy who looked like he went to Yale or Harvard or some big-time college. It was summer, and he had on a white shirt with a bow tie. He spoke up in a proper voice, saying, "I'm the only guy in this class. I don't want these other guys taking my place, Ms. Ana. I studied my lines too hard. There is no way they can speak clearly and feel the character like I can."

Ms. Ana smiled at him and said something that she must have thought was way over our heads. "You have nothing to worry about, my dear boy. Besides, they're amateurs. You don't need to be intimidated by these boys. I'm sure they don't have the work ethic in them that you have."

"Is she trying to say that we can't learn this acting stuff?" Antoine leaned over and asked me. "Huh. Whatever that little stuffy dude can do, I can do better."

Now that he saw his competition, Antoine was suddenly into this acting class. I still wasn't convinced it was for me, but Mom wanted me to come here. She must have thought it was a good idea. So I wasn't going to be mean to Ms. Ana even though she was being mean to us.

For the rest of the day, Ms. Ana really ignored us and worked with the other three actors. The tall girl, the boy wearing the bow tie, and another girl were getting all the attention. At first, the other girl was real quiet, but she kept staring at me. Antoine must have thought she was kind of pretty because he kept looking at her.

Around noon, we stopped for a lunch break. When lunchtime was almost over, Antoine walked up to the girl. He wanted to introduce himself, but she walked around him and held out her hand to me. "I'm Sasha. What's your name?"

"He's nobody. I'm his big brother, Antoine," he said, as he tried to grab her hand.

"What? Please! You've been trying to show off all morning. And just like Ms. Ana isn't paying you any attention, I'm not paying you any attention either. What's your name?" she asked me again.

"We're not done," Antoine said, as he stormed away.

"Hi. I'm Alec, and that was my brother, Antoine. You know, you just made him wanna bug you even more."

Just then Ms. Ana called out to us. "Okay, let's practice being farm animals. Antoine, I want you to be a pig. Now, on the count of three, assume your role. One . . . Two—"

Antoine cut her off. "I'm not bein' a pig! Let him do it," he said rudely, pointing at the other boy.

"I asked you to do it," said Ms. Ana.

She had already told Antoine that she liked his strong personality, and now he was taking advantage of that. He wanted her to know he was tough and he wasn't going to do just anything she said.

But Ms. Ana was tougher. "Now, listen hear, young man. You don't run my theater company. If you don't want to do what I tell you to do, then go and sit on the very last seat in the back and wait until your mother comes to pick you up."

Antoine said, "No problem with me. I don't wanna be here anyway."

Ms. Ana replied, "It's good to have a big personality, but it's not good to be disrespectful. And, don't worry, you won't be allowed to come back again."

I didn't like that my brother wouldn't be able to participate. Sure, he was a little hotheaded, but this was our first time here. And she wasn't making it easy. Ms. Ana wasn't calling on us to do the cool stuff. Who could fault him for not wanting to do the corny stuff?

So I went up to her and said, "Excuse me, Ms. Ana, . . . um—"

She cut me off. "Young man, don't interrupt me in the middle of my session again. Go and sit down beside your brother."

"Ma'am, what did I do?"

"Earth to Alec!" she said a little too loudly. "Are you not listening? You interrupted me, and you were trying to tell me how to lead my workshop. Now go and sit down."

"Man, you stood up for me?" Antoine said when I sat next to him.

I was so angry. If he would have put up with what the lady asked him to do and acted like a pig the way she wanted him to, neither of us would be sitting down. But Antoine didn't make me take up for him. So I couldn't be that mad at him. I just think she took it too far.

"Thanks, man. That was cool. I'll handle things with Mom so both of us won't be in trouble."

"Naw, I don't wanna come back either. Both of us can be in trouble."

We just laughed. An hour later, the time was over.

Sasha came up to me and said, "Don't worry. She'll get over it, and tomorrow will be a better day. She acts tough but she's not really so bad."

When Mom came in to get us, she asked, "Okay, why are you two sitting down?"

We both turned around to see Ms. Ana walking toward

us. She didn't waste any time telling Mom, "I don't want them back."

Mom looked disappointed with Ms. Ana and annoyed with us. We had been trying to please her, but we had let her down. She didn't like hearing that we were out. It was a mess.

● ● ●

"You know what, you don't need to walk off from me. And you're not going to put my kids out of your program." Mom shocked both me and Antoine as she spoke to Ms. Ana.

The other three kids were gone, so it was just the four of us there, and Mom wasn't holding back her tongue. Even so, her angry words didn't seem to be getting to Ms. Ana because she hadn't turned around. She kept walking away and wasn't paying Mom any attention.

As we stood there watching her put props away, I said to our mother, "Mom, we really don't want to do this anymore. We tried it, but it didn't work out. I guess it's just not for us, so it's no big deal if she doesn't want us around."

Mom was really annoyed and couldn't hold back her frustration. "Alec, please, we'll be leaving in just a minute. I just need you and your brother to wait over there. Okay?"

"Yeah, let's wait over here," said Antoine, pulling me back because he was happy to see my mother argue with somebody.

I said to him, "You know this isn't right."

Antoine grinned and asked me, "What do you mean?"

"We should try to move our mom away from an argument, not push her to it. That lady is twice her age."

"So what? She thinks she's all that. No way she's gonna kick us out of her program. I'm glad to see Mom stand up for us. I haven't seen her act this way in a long time. I remember once I had a teacher who called me dumb when we moved to a new school. Mom went up there and told her, 'Don't ever tell my son that he's dumb.'"

"But you weren't really trying and that teacher was right."

"I know, but still it felt good seeing Mom take up for me. All teachers aren't bad. Most of them care, but every now and then you get someone like Ms. Ana who needs to be reminded."

I just rolled my eyes. My brother was different from me. I wanted peace and he didn't.

Then we heard Ms. Ana tell Mom, "This is my program, Lisa, and I can do whatever I want. I can teach whomever I want. And since you aren't paying anyway . . . "

Mom shot back, "You wouldn't take my money! What are you talking about?"

"Right, because my mama got money to pay. You tell her, Mom," Antoine said out loud.

"My kids are here for the summer. I really wanted you to spend some time with them and get to know them. I thought you would want that too."

"Why does she want this lady to get to know us?" I said to Antoine.

"Hhhumm uhh," was all he could say.

"I have a busy shooting schedule. I just don't want them home alone all day. I know you, you're stubborn, but you can at least spend a little time with them. It won't be for long."

"Where does Mom know this lady from?" I asked Antoine.

"Who cares? Shhh! I can't hear what they're sayin'."

"It's adult talk. You shouldn't be listening anyway."

"Whatever. They could go to another room, but they're talking right in front of us. So I'm gonna check it out. The only thing I'm missin' is some popcorn and a soda."

"This is not a show, Antoine."

"Boy, please, this is the best entertainment in town. All I need is a camera. I could produce a reality show with this material."

"You? A producer? Since when did you start thinking about that?"

"We're in Hollywood, baby! Who wouldn't want to check this out? There's an angle here. Mom, the actress, and the acting coach goin' at it."

Then Mom said, "So you're not going to bend. You're not going to apologize to my boys?"

"They're just kids. Do I look like I'm going to apologize to them?"

"You know what . . . I don't even know why I tried.

Come on, guys. Let's go," Mom said, as she turned and walked away from Ms. Ana.

Mom was clearly angry, but somehow it felt like she was hurt on top of that.

"So that's it? You're just going to walk out of my life again!" Ms. Ana said to our mother before we got to the door. She surprised all three of us.

I looked up at Mom and saw that she had tears in her eyes, and I knew something else was bothering her. Then, she started to let it all out.

"When I decided I was going to get married, you weren't there for me. When I had my babies, you weren't there. And now that I'm back on TV, you find me again and tell me how much you miss me and how much you want to be a part of my life. But because I didn't have enough time to come inside and introduce you to my kids . . . because of my job that you so badly want me to have . . . you got mad and act this way, Mom?"

Antoine was standing there with his mouth wide open. My face was all crunched up in amazement. This lady, this mean person, this acting coach, was my grandmother? My mother never talked about her family. Dad's mom was always around, taking care of us when we needed her.

But since we never talked about our mother's mom, I guess I thought she wasn't alive. I never wanted to bring it up because I was afraid I'd hurt her feelings or something. But to find out suddenly that she'd been alive all this time and didn't want to be with us made me feel sick to my stomach.

"Antoine, close your mouth," Mom told him.

"Man, I'm just like trippin'. You mean, this is your mom? No wonder we're so much alike. Wow! So I'm not just some person who's different from you, Dad, and Alec. I'm like somebody else in our family. Somebody actually gets me. This is so cool!"

To me, Antoine was talking very weird and it was confusing. When I looked at my grandmother's face, although she was trying to hide her feelings, she was pleased. But, for my mom and me, this wasn't cool at all. Antoine might be proud to be like her, but I was glad I wasn't like Ms. Ana. I was like our mother. I didn't like the fact that Mom needed her at times when she wasn't there.

So quickly, I prayed, *"Lord, this is hard news to hear. Am I supposed to love this lady, and I don't understand her?"*

I walked over to Ms. Ana and asked, "You're my grandmother? You were really going to put us out of your program. Don't you love us?"

She just looked at me. Mom reached for me and hugged me tight. "I love you, baby. Come on. Let's get out of here. It was my fault. I should have told you guys, but I was rushing, and I just didn't know how to break the news. I was hoping my mother would welcome you. Oh, this is so hard."

"Keep running. Keep going. Don't deal with it. Even though your son just asked a question, and I want to answer it."

"Okay, Mom. You talk to them. You tell them about when I left California to start a family and how you thought I was making the worst mistake of my life. You tell my kids how wrong I was."

Antoine went over to her and said, "It's okay. Talk to my brother. Tell him how you feel about him. Alec is used to it. He's lived with me all his life. Just be honest."

Our grandmother finally gave in. "Okay. Okay. I admit it. I made some mistakes, but I do love you boys, and I love my daughter. It hurts me that I haven't been there for you guys, but I'm just simply not like most grandparents, nor do I think I'm alone. There are lots of people who aren't touchy-feely. I'm not the only one who doesn't act all warm and fuzzy."

When she paused for a minute, Antoine told her, "Yeah, we get it. Keep going."

"And when my daughter left California, although I have family here, a big part of me was gone. Instead of agreeing with her decision, I became bitter. She's one of the best actresses I know. Her old show had gotten picked up because of her, and I didn't want her to give that up for anything. But when I look at you two boys, I see she gave it up for everything. You're quite amazing. Antoine, I do see a lot of me in you and that's something," our grandmother explained.

Then she turned to me and said something I was glad to hear. Grandma Ana said, "And you, Mr. Alec, you've got a big heart just like your mother. Where'd the years go? If I had them back, I'd do things differently. I would be there for all of you. I do want you to come back tomorrow. I do want to get to know you. So what do you say?"

Antoine went right up to her and hugged her. I just stood back and stared, holding on to Mom's hand. Taking all of this in was a big deal.

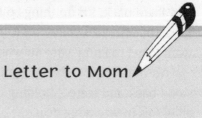

Letter to Mom

Dear Mom,

What an awesome condo you have. It's cozy and beautiful. I see why you don't want to come home. I'm just kidding. I thought I was past letting Antoine get to me, but I still get upset with him sometimes. One minute he does something that I admire, then the next thing I know he's acting all bossy.

Thank you for allowing me to explain myself no matter what the situation. I feel like I can talk to you about anything. I'm not sure about acting. I know Antoine and I are amateurs and Ms. Ana made us feel pretty bad. I was really shocked to find out that she is our grandma. Mom, she doesn't seem anything like you.

Your son,
Uncomfortable Alec

Word Search: Division I Teams

In the world of college athletics, baseball is a very important sport. Hidden in the puzzle, find some of the colleges and universities that usually lead the way in this sport.

```
K  P  M  A  I  N  I  G  R  I  V  A
F  L  M  Y  N  R  V  G  E  G  R  B
M  D  U  H  L  I  C  H  V  I  W  F
A  T  Y  W  T  C  L  R  Z  Y  G  O
N  V  D  R  L  E  L  O  T  A  T  H
B  T  R  B  I  L  N  E  R  F  V  M
S  M  O  K  L  A  H  O  M  A  G  F
C  B  F  O  S  L  G  I  T  S  C  Y
L  T  N  T  M  U  B  R  X  E  O  S
D  A  A  H  H  P  O  G  T  E  G  N
A  T  T  Z  A  Z  D  E  L  H  X  A
E  R  S  Q  B  E  G  S  N  V  K  F
```

ARIZONASTATE   CLEMSON   OKLAHOMA   RICE
(Arizona State)

SCAROLINA   STANFORD   VIRGINIA
(South Carolina)

Proud
Actor

6

"**Mom, I just** don't understand why you never told us about our grandmother. I mean, don't you think that's important to know?" Antoine asked at dinner later that evening.

Antoine and I were still in shock that we had met our mom's mother. We couldn't stop talking about the grandmother we never knew we had. Mom looks like her but they have different personalities. Grandma Ana is definitely full of energy. Antoine acts just like her, and because I'm more like Mom, I act totally different. It's strange to me that, even though my brother and I look different from each other, we both look like our grandmother.

Sitting at the table, Mom was looking all teary-eyed and her hands were shaking. All of our questions seemed hard for her, but Antoine and I wanted to know. Even though the memories were painful for her, we needed to know. I reached across the table to grab her hand. She dropped her fork on her plate and grabbed my hand back.

Mom took another deep breath and closed her eyes. "Okay, boys, I know we have to talk. I remember when you guys were little, you used to ask about my mom. I didn't want to talk about her, so I gave you a lot of excuses. To be honest, my mother and I had a big disagreement when I was younger, so we became estranged. Do you know what that means?"

"Yeah," I said. "It's when two people don't wanna talk to each other or see each other anymore. But why was she mad that you wanted to be with us?"

Wiping her eyes, she said, "It all started before you both were born. She wasn't ready for me to get married and have a family. My mother was very unhappy that I left the world she had helped me to build. You see, in her younger years, my mother wanted to be an actress and it just didn't work out for her. When she had me, she invested everything into making me a big star. But I was a scared little girl who wasn't ready for the Hollywood life. I wanted to get away from that whole situation. My mother kept pushing me from audition to audition. But I just wanted to be normal. I just wanted to enjoy life my way. Then, I went to college, met your dad, and the rest is history. My mom didn't approve. She told me to leave and never look back."

"Your mom said that?" I asked.

"Yes, some pretty harsh words, right? She definitely gave me tough love. Although, I have to say that I did become fond of acting after awhile. I just had to do it in my own timing. Look, you boys are growing up now. Mom has always had her own way of thinking. You can tell that she is a lot to deal with. Now she sees that the time she spent pushing me away from her is gone forever. She couldn't forgive me for not doing things the way she wanted. I think she realizes now that not only was she hurting me, she was hurting herself as well."

The more she talked it out with us, I think Mom was beginning to feel a little better. Her tears stopped falling, and it seemed easier for her to talk. "I have to say, after I became a mother, I understood a lot of what she felt back then. That's why I want the best for you guys, even though I'm far away from you. I know it's a bit out of the ordinary that your mother isn't with you all the time, but know that you are always in my heart. I pray for you boys every day. I also need to make sure that my mom is a part of our lives. Just like you're spending time with your father's mother, you boys need time to get to know my mother too."

"And, Ms. Ana," Antoine added, "she's cool."

"Yep, Ms. Ana," Mom smiled and said, "She's something else. I figured you would like her, Antoine. You all are like two peas in a pod."

"I mean, what can I say?" Antoine said proudly. He was grinning and playing with his pretend beard.

"If it's too much for you, I don't want to press you boys into getting to know my mother right now. I was busy this morning, but I have to admit, a part of me didn't want to introduce you guys. I guess I wanted to see how you would connect before you knew who she was. I don't know, maybe that was the wrong way to handle it," Mom said sadly, as she held her head down.

"You don't have to explain, Mom," I said to her. I got up, lifted her chin, and then gave her a big hug.

"And, yeah, we wanna know her," Antoine said. "We're goin' back tomorrow, right?"

Before she could answer, the doorbell rang. When Antoine opened the door, a man who looked like a grown up version of my brother walked in. "Oh, Lisa! This boy looks like me," he said.

"Granddad?" Antoine asked unsure of what to say.

Mom laughed as Grandma Ana and another lady walked in next. The lady was carrying a basket with a checkered red and white handkerchief covering it. They were laughing too.

Mom got up from the table and went to greet her guests. "Antoine, no," she started, as she hugged the man. "This is Uncle Jack. Hey, Uncle Jack."

"Hey, baby girl," Uncle Jack said back. I could see from the proud look on his face that he was real happy to see my mother.

I kept looking at Uncle Jack. It seemed like I knew him. But from where?

Finally, Mom said, "Stop staring at my mom's brother, Alec, and speak to everyone."

"Do I know him?" I asked, trying not to stare anymore.

"Yes, you do. He's a big time actor. You've seen him on TV," she said, feeling proud and glad that I recognized him.

"And comedian. Don't forget that, Miss Lisa," Uncle Jack added. To my surprise, he pretended like he was trying to pick up my mom. But he was acting like he couldn't because she was too heavy. That was funny. Then he turned to Antoine and me and said, "So who do we have here?"

"I'm Antoine."

"And I'm Alec," I said, while reaching out to shake his hand.

Uncle Jack teased, "Wow. Yeah, y'all are definitely related to me. Some handsome young men you've got, Lisa."

"Hah! In your dreams you look so good. I definitely don't agree with that," said Grandma Ana. "Thank goodness, the boys take after me."

"Whatever, Ana," Uncle Jack replied. "Boys, this is my wife. Say hello to your aunt Jan."

We waved and said hello. Aunt Jan smiled and said, "Hi, boys. I brought you some cookies and muffins."

"She loves to bake," said Uncle Jack.

"Eat up, boys," Aunt Jan urged us. The sweet smell of the treats filled the air when she lifted the napkin.

We glanced at our mom for permission. "You've finished your dinner. Go ahead and help yourself."

"Thank you, ma'am," I said to Aunt Jan, as I dug in.

"Yeah, thanks so much. These are delicious," Antoine

said, after gobbling his second cookie down in a flash.

"Oh, you're welcome. And what nice manners you have," replied Aunt Jan.

"I told Jack we should have come over here on another day but he just couldn't wait to see you and the boys," Grandma said to Mom.

Grandma Ana seemed just as excited as Uncle Jack and Aunt Jan to see us. In fact, she was smiling so hard I could see that she had a dimple in her cheek. It was cool. We were happy to see all of them too!

"It's okay, Mom. We're glad you came."

"Aren't they some fine young men, Jack?" asked Grandma Ana.

"Yep! They're my blood. Come on over here, boys, so Uncle Jack can make your pockets fat," he said, pulling out a wad of one-hundred-dollar bills.

"Uncle Jack, I can't let you give that to the boys," Mom protested.

"Oh please, child. Do you know how many birthdays I've missed out on? We'll just call this back pay. I'm making up for lost time."

"Yeah, Mom. He's makin' up for lost time," Antoine said with both his hands out.

Mom slapped his hands down. "No thanks, Uncle Jack, they don't need it."

"Speak for yourself, Mom. I do need it!"

"Antoine, what did I just say?"

"Aw, okay then. Man!" Antoine said, backing off.

As for me, I was in awe at the moment, watching my family interacting with each other. I just looked to the ceiling and said a prayer, *"Lord, I thank You. I'm just so thankful to have a grandma and a great uncle and aunt who care about us. We're family, and they love us. Thank You for loving us so much. Yeah, it was tough having Mom leave us and work in California, but now it's okay, 'cause I can clearly see, You got me."*

● ● ●

"Dad!" I shouted when I saw my father and ran to him. We had come to meet him at the airport.

"Hey, Alec! Give me a big hug. I missed ya, man."

"I missed you too."

I was so glad to see Dad that I couldn't sleep the night before. It wasn't like my father was in the armed forces like Morgan's dad and had been gone for months at a time. Two weeks was long enough for us to not see him. We were used to joking around with Dad every day, and I really missed that. It felt great seeing him again.

"Hey, Dad! Antoine came running up to our father and gave him a big hug.

"Hi, son! Long time, no see," Dad said with a big smile and hug. "So you boys are cool with the fact that I'm not going to hang out with you and your brother this weekend? You know, I came to spend some time with your mom."

"Yeah, Dad. You guys have a good time." Then I pulled him closer so I could whisper in his ear, "Between you and me, I know she misses you."

"Thanks, man. I guess you guys have been having some good times with your grandma, huh?"

Mom was standing back taking it all in. She was smiling with the biggest smile ever! I guess this was the way she felt the first time she ever met Dad.

Antoine was happy too. He was skipping around in circles for no reason. Dad grabbed him, and they hugged real tight.

"I see you found your twin," Dad said, as he motioned toward Grandma.

"It's cool," said Antoine, grinning from ear to ear.

But the look on Grandma Ana's face wasn't such a pleasant one. I could tell that she and Dad weren't fond of each other because they weren't hiding it from anyone.

"Yeah, we've been having a lot of fun with Grandma," I said, needing him to cut her some slack.

Then Dad hugged my mom so big and tight, she lifted off of her feet. "I missed you, Lisa."

"I missed you too, Andre. And I want you and my mom to play nice. Okay?" I could tell Mom wasn't playing. She looked both of them in the eye when she said that.

Barely with a smile, he turned to Grandma and said, "Ana."

"Andre," Grandma said back with a little chill like on a windy spring day. "You both go on and enjoy yourselves. We'll see you on Sunday. Boys, say your good-byes."

Although I was super glad that my parents were getting

along, I didn't want us to be apart. I couldn't help but think about how much fun the four of us could have at Disney World or at Sea World. Knowing Dad, he would probably even want to take us to a Dodgers game. Those were the kinds of things I'd been wishing for, but we could experience them later. Now, it was time to hug them both and part ways with my parents. Leaving the airport with my brother and grandma, I knew Mom and Dad needed some time together—just the two of them.

"I thought they would never leave. C'mon, we've got somewhere to go," Grandma Ana said in a hurried voice.

"Where are we goin'?" Antoine asked.

"Well, here's the thing. You guys have been going to my acting sessions for the past two weeks and both of you are showing improvement. You know, stars in the making, just like your mom. Now, I want to take you to an audition for a PSA. Do you know what that is?"

"Yes, ma'am. It's a public service announcement," I answered.

"Alec, good job."

Quickly, I said, "But I don't want to be in a commercial."

"Speak for yourself," said Antoine. "I do, Grandma."

"Good, baby. I'm head of a major talent agency, and I signed both of you up. You don't have to like it, but try it out anyway. You don't have to like spinach, but you've gotta eat it to grow strong. Just like Popeye. Catch my drift?"

"Like who?"

Grandma frowned and repeated, "Popeye. He's a character from an old cartoon. I can't believe you guys don't know about Popeye. Anyway, I don't want any grumbling or mumbling. You will audition."

There was no way to escape this. Grandma was serious, and she meant business. We drove for a while and then pulled up to the studio lot. To make sure I wasn't dreaming, I had to keep blinking my eyes. It was an amazing place.

Antoine and I had seen lots of TV shows and movies, but we'd never been on an actual lot. We saw huge trucks carrying camera equipment and crews around. Everywhere we looked people were busy rushing back and forth. We peeked inside trailers where actors were getting made up. Rows and rows of all kinds of bright and colorful costumes were everywhere we looked.

Antoine was alert and ready for action. I wasn't ready to try out. I had knots in my stomach that felt like spiders crawling around inside me. But Grandma had already told me I couldn't back out, so I had to think of something that made me want to go through with it.

All of a sudden, I had it! I thought about how excited I felt after I hit the baseball for the first time. At first, I didn't wanna walk up to the plate when I was trying to learn how to play. After a few tries, I could finally walk up to the ball, swing at it, and hit it.

So I tried to do the same with the script they gave me.

But every time I looked at it, all I could do was stare at the page. Grandma saw that I was frozen, and she came over to me. I thought she was about to scold me, but for the first time she acted like a real grandmother. She was sensitive and not stern. Kind of reminding me of Mom, Grandma was calm and concerned.

"I know this is a little scary and different for you. But Alec, you're tough. You're good. Give it your best shot, just like we talked about in acting class. Think about what the character would be doing. Remember, this isn't about you. It's about bullying. Can you relate to that?"

When I heard that word, my mind quickly went back to second grade. I used to bully people and make them feel uneasy. Then, in the fourth grade, I met Tyrod, and he acted like bullying was his middle name. It made me want the whole idea of bullying to be stopped.

So I thought, *Okay. Yeah, I could make a PSA about this.* I was ready. I knew I could do a great job too.

Two hours later, Grandma came to me, bubbling over with excitement. "Oh my goodness, you're not going to believe this!"

Antoine stepped in front of me and said, "What? I got the role?"

She smiled, patted him on the head, and said, "No honey, your brother did."

He was furious. I didn't even want the part, but I got it. What was I going to do now?

● ● ●

"Okay, Alec. Get on up, honey. I know you can't wait to tape the PSA," Grandma Ana said early the next morning. It was the happiest voice I ever heard her speak in.

Really, I wasn't excited at all about going to the PSA taping. It was four o'clock in the morning, and I had to get up this early to make call time on the set. I didn't get any sleep overnight. To make it even worse, Antoine cried during the night. He didn't think I heard him, but I did. I know it was hard for him that I beat him out on something he wanted and I didn't even want to do. We had gotten pretty cool now, and I didn't want this to come between us.

California had really been good for all of us. Although we had to leave Dad at home, for the first time in a long time we were with our mom every day. Now Mom and Dad were having a chance to be together and that was cool too. On top of all that, being in a new and different place had allowed Antoine and me to bond like never before.

I knew that doing this commercial meant a lot more to Antoine than to me. If I could gain more points with Antoine by letting him go in my place, then that's what I would do.

"Come on, baby, get up. Oh, look, you're sweating," Grandma said to me, as she pulled back the covers.

And then it dawned on me. I could play sick! She said I was a good actor, so I figured I could start acting now.

I moaned and grumbled, "Grandma. My head. My stomach. I don't feel well."

Panicking, she said, "Oh, no! Let me go and get the thermometer. You can't be sick. We've got to get out of here."

Just as she left the room, I looked over at Antoine. Like me, he was usually sleeping hard this early in the morning, but his eyes met mine. He wasn't sleeping at all.

He'd been listening and asked me in a worried tone, "What's wrong with you? You all right, Alec?"

Antoine got up and came over to my bed. I was really happy that he cared if I was ill, but I didn't want him to get too close to me. He would know I was faking. I was sweating because I had the covers pulled over my face and head. Antoine was pretty smart, and he'd size me up in a minute if I let down my guard.

After I jerked away a few times, he was determined to touch my forehead. "You're not hot!"

"Shhh!" I said. "Just go with the flow. Work with me."

"Work with you on what?"

"I'm playin' sick."

"Why? You know you don't have much time until you have to be on the set."

I didn't say anything. I just rolled over in frustration. If only he understood.

"Wait a minute, Alec. You're doin' this for me?"

"Yeah. You're the one who wanted this."

"I'm all right. You beat me fair and square. It's not a big deal."

"It *is* a big deal, Antoine. I heard you all night."

"You ain't heard nothin'."

Trying to get him to understand where I was coming from, I said, "Whatever, man. I know I heard crying all night. This is me. Your brother, Alec. I know you. And I don't wanna do the shoot. You'll do great. The director just didn't give you a chance. I probably got the role because I dealt with bullying at my school. Believe me bullying isn't a good thing at all. You're probably the only one who thinks Tyrod is actually cool. But he's a bully, and no one wants to have him around."

"I hear you, bro, but you can do a great job on the commercial too. Do it."

Grandma Ana walked in with a thermometer. "Get back from him, Antoine. Let him breathe. He could be contagious, and you could catch it. Turn over so I can take your temperature, Alec."

"Oh, no!" I called out when she motioned for me to roll onto my back.

"I can't believe this is happening to me. I finally get a big chance. I finally get a client to select my talent from the agency and now he's sick. You've got to go, Alec. I hope you don't have a fever."

I backed up to the wall. I didn't want her to check my temperature. Shaking my head no, I pointed over at my brother. I wanted her to take Antoine instead.

"What? I can't just take someone else. It's not that simple," she said, as I frowned even more.

"You heard, Grandma. I can't go in your place.

Grandma, nothing is wrong with him," Antoine said, as he took the pillow and lightly threw it in my face.

"What do you mean, nothing is wrong with him? Boy, if you don't get up from that bed and get dressed. We should have left twenty minutes ago. Now, hurry up!"

When she left the room to get ready, I said, "Why won't you just do it? The reason I want you to tape the commercial is so you won't be mad at me."

"We're cool, Alec. I don't wanna take anything away from you. I want to earn stuff my way. I did my thing in baseball, and that blew me away. I know my time will come again. It might be in acting or maybe something else. I got my act together in basketball. Right now, I wanna have your back. It's kinda cool that you were willing to give it all up for me, though. I give you props for that."

We did a high-five and then quickly got dressed. Antoine wasn't going to miss the taping. He was right there with me. Even though I was nervous, he cheered me on from the sidelines. It was time for me to step outside my comfort zone. The director told me when I was supposed to speak, and I nailed every line the way I needed to.

By the end of the first few takes, I was beginning to enjoy acting. It wasn't so bad after all. Deep down, I was really pleased to shoot the public service announcement. And if I was asked to film one again, I'd gladly do it and be a proud actor.

Letter to Mom

Dear Mom,

What a surprise you and your mom gave us. I think it was so cool to meet our grandmother. She is a strong, cool lady. I was sorry to hear you all have been estranged. But I'm glad to see the two of you get back together again.

Coming to California was the best thing that could happen to us this summer. It was good to meet Uncle Jack and Aunt Jan too. I'm happy to know that we have family who love us. That makes me very proud.

Your son,
Happy Alec

Word Search: HBCU Teams

HISTORICALLY BLACK COLLEGES AND UNIVERSITY TEAMS

There are four major HBCU athletic conferences. They are the Southern Intercollegiate Athletic Conference (SIAC), Mid-Eastern Athletic Conference (MEAC), Southwestern Athletic Conference (SWAC), and the Central Intercollegiate Athletic Association (CIAA). Below are some of the top schools that are great in the sport of baseball. Find them in the puzzle.

```
G  A  T  J  Z  Y  K  C  F  M  A  E
T  L  K  S  N  A  Q  O  P  I  L  L
S  C  U  W  Y  M  Q  V  F  L  A  O
K  O  O  C  E  N  U  H  T  E  B  J
L  R  U  Y  C  J  A  U  H  S  A  M
O  N  A  T  L  T  B  B  S  O  M  F
F  S  K  O  H  O  B  W  L  R  A  U
R  T  R  H  Q  E  O  T  F  A  A  U
O  L  C  H  J  T  R  L  V  I  M  H
N  W  W  V  J  W  A  N  U  F  Q  H
F  E  B  G  M  V  C  F  J  U  M  K
X  A  G  D  I  J  J  P  O  I  Z  U
```

ALABAMAAM (Alabama A&M) **ALBANYST** (Albany State) **ALCORNST** (Alcorn State) **BETHUNECOOK** (Bethune Cookman)

MILES **NORFOLKST** (Norfolk State) **SOUTHERN**

115

Wonderful
Outcome

7

"**Hey, Grandma. You're** here?" I said in a surprised tone when I opened up my mom's apartment door.

However, instead of giving me a hug, she put her finger over her lips and said, "Shhh! Where's your mom?"

I could tell right away that Grandma was up to something. Now I was convinced where Antoine got it from. He was just like her.

"She's in the kitchen on a call."

"Where's your brother?"

"He's in our room playing a video game."

She pointed toward our bedroom and whispered that we needed to go in there with Antoine.

"Now be quiet and hurry," she ordered.

I didn't know what she was up to, but I went along with her. When we got in the room, Grandma shut the door quietly. She tapped Antoine on the shoulder. He was so into the game that he didn't notice we were behind him.

But before he could make any noise, she covered his mouth.

She said, "Shhh. Quiet, I have some great news, but we need to keep it under wraps."

"Is it about the audition I went on last week? They want me to come back, right?" asked Antoine. His eyes were wider than a deer staring into some bright headlights.

Last week, Grandma also took us to audition for Disney. For years, we've watched the Disney TV channel, but being under those studio lights was something magical. They took us on a tour, and we saw where some of our favorite shows were taped. Lights, cameras, and stars were everywhere. I remember that it gave Antoine and me the feeling that anything was possible.

I knew that Antoine really wanted to land a Disney show gig. That news would really make his day. Grandma reached out her hand and touched his shoulder. "Not this time, baby, but I'm looking into something for you," she reassured him.

He asked, "Then, what's the great news?"

She turned to me and said, "Alec, you have a callback for the show, and I have a good feeling that you're going to get it."

It was kind of weird because inside I was jumping with joy. I mean, not too long ago I didn't want anything to do with television acting, but now I was pumped up. I did well enough to get a call back, and she thought I actually had a chance at getting a role. I was over-the-top excited, but I could see Antoine's face drop. He looked so sad.

I honestly believed if I did get it, it would hurt him badly. We only had a couple of days before we would be headed back home. I certainly didn't want to do anything to break us apart again. I really loved my brother. Now that we were close, I didn't want our bond to be broken.

"Alec, you don't seem excited. This is a great opportunity. Don't worry. I'll find something for Antoine."

My brother turned and said, "Yeah, don't worry about me, bro, you gotta do this. I've just got to step up my game. I'm not mad at you. All right? Go finish strong and get on that show."

It was such a good feeling to see that Antoine's attitude toward me was changing for the better. After my brother gave me that little pep talk, I looked at Grandma and said, "Okay, I'm ready. Let's go and tell Mom the news."

She grabbed the back of my shirt and said, "Wait, wait, wait. No, no, no. You need to get the gig first and then tell your mom. She doesn't need to know about this right now. So Antoine, I need you to cover for us."

I squinted at her because I wasn't comfortable with keeping this a secret from my mother. "I don't understand why Mom can't know. She's an actress. She might want to come and help me."

Right away, Grandma got mad and raised her voice. "I said she doesn't need to know about this audition right now. Let's just go. We can't be late!"

Then it happened. When Grandma turned toward the

door, she was face to face with Mom.

Standing in the doorway, Mom demanded, "Where are you taking Alec?"

"Umm, uhh . . . " Grandma said, stumbling over her words.

"Mom, what's going on?" my mom asked, putting her hand on her hip. "You're not trying to take my son to an audition, are you?"

"You don't even understand, Lisa. This is a big one. It could change his whole life. If Alec lands this one, he'll be set for good. I think he has a very good chance too. I've already spoken to the producer and they really, really like him. It's a callback for D-I-S-N-E-Y," she said, spelling the name out. I guess she thought that would make a difference with Mom.

Throwing up her hands in frustration, Mom said, "I don't care if it's for the president."

"Why, Mom? I wanna go," I pleaded.

"See, now look what you've done. When Andre and I got back from San Francisco last week, you told us about the PSA. We were okay with that, but we told you bottom line that we didn't want our boys involved in any of this Hollywood stuff. That was my life. You put me in that. I can't have you do the same to my kids."

"Yes, I did . . . are you telling me that you regret I made you a star?"

"I'm telling you that I missed out on a lot of my child-hood because of it, and I don't want my kids to lose out on theirs. My boys are about to go back to Georgia so they can get ready for school. My son is not staying out here to be on TV."

I said, "But, Mom—"

"Son, you're going to have to trust me on this. Being a child star is a tough life. If you think you might really want to be an actor one day, you need to listen to me. If and when the time is right, we'll know."

Both Antoine and I didn't like what she was saying. Neither did our grandmother. Her eyes had turned red and watery. But at the end of the discussion, Mom got to decide.

But Grandma wouldn't give up. Trying to be nice, she said in a sweet tone, "I can't believe you're going to let this boy miss out on such a great opportunity. Both of your sons are talented. They need to stay out here."

"Mother, you don't have to like my decision. Neither do my boys, but its final. You guys are going to have to respect it. Antoine, Alec, believe me. It's what's best."

I didn't think so, but there was nothing I could do about it. She had spoken, and I had to live with it. For now, my big dream of becoming a star was crushed—and I wasn't happy about it.

● ● ●

It was my last day in Hollywood, and I was in a bad mood. Mom had not only killed Grandma's dreams of working with her grandsons to make us actors, but she had put the brakes on her own children's hopes and ambitions. So what, she regretted being a child star? How did she know we'd regret it?

I watched Disney, Nickelodeon, Cartoon Network, and Public Broadcasting TV all the time. I've seen tons of young kids on those channels doing their thing. Besides, Mom herself always commented that there needs to be more African American representation on kids TV shows. If she would have just let me respond to the callback, then maybe I could have helped to change that.

"Boys, hurry up and get ready," Mom said to us. She peeked into our room and saw we were moping and packing very slowly.

"But, Mom, the plane doesn't leave until later this evening," Antoine said to her.

She replied, "We're going to church first."

About an hour later, we were seated at New Mercies Christian Church. This was our fourth Sunday in California and the first time visiting church. I guess Mom wanted that to change before we left.

"Good afternoon, everyone. Thank you for joining us on this fantastic Youth Sunday. I'm the youth pastor, J.C. Brown, and today I'm excited to bring you a word from the Lord. I want to talk to you about the subject, 'Going the Distance.'"

People in the audience started *oohhing* and *aahhing*. I looked at Antoine and he looked back at me. We didn't get it. Okay, going the distance . . . what was the big deal?

"I can tell that some of you guys feel me," said Rev. Brown. "Young people tend to quit on a whole lot of things. They quit on their school lessons, and they quit on doing their homework. Sadly, sometimes they quit on their dreams. I stand before you today because I believe that the hopes and dreams many young people leave behind can be fulfilled. You see, when you stay focused and keep the right attitude, with a desire to please God—you will reach your goals. Now, how many of you here, adults too, get upset, frustrated, and angry when things don't go your way?"

At that moment, I wanted to slide down in the pew because I'd been acting really disappointed over the last couple of days. Mom had told me I couldn't try out for the part and be an actor at this point in my life. She said that I had to go back to Georgia and keep doing well in school. I'd been definitely showing how upset I was about it.

Rev. Brown then said, "Young people, we've got to change our mind-set. We've got to change our way of thinking. In 1 Corinthians, chapter 9, verses 24–27, the apostle Paul is talking about running the race of life in such a way as to get the ultimate prize. He explains that, in a race, all the runners run—but only one gets the prize. That person is the one who did the best. Now, take a minute and think about a track race."

I did just that and imagined myself on a track. I'm bent down like the runners I watched in the Olympics. As soon as they heard the signal, they took off like the wind.

Remembering how exciting it was to watch them made me want to try track one day.

Rev. Brown continued the sermon, "Life is like a track meet. Every time I've watched one, I've never seen a runner quit. Some might fall and have to stop, but they don't just give up. They keep running toward the finish line. They want to be the first to cross the tape because they know that only one person can be number one and win. In fact, life is like any sporting event when teams are competing. They don't stop, and they don't give up. They want to win. They want to become the champs. Young people, we must learn not give up on ourselves so easily and strive to be champions for God."

I was listening. I was taking in every word. I wanted to make God proud, but how?

The answer came when Rev. Brown said, "Sometimes things happen in life that you don't like. Pray about those things and ask for God's help. But, don't get an attitude because you don't think you're being treated fairly. You've got a God in heaven who loves you. As long as you stay focused on Him, God will help you overcome your stress and worries.

Yes, there are many lessons in life that you will have to learn along the way. You won't always get to have it your way. Sometimes things will happen that you won't agree with. You may not like everything that you have to go through, but that doesn't mean that you should quit trying. These are important lessons to learn. So take something powerful away from this Youth Day. When you're faced with a hard test, try even harder and do your best. Be prepared to go the distance in everything you do. Make God proud."

Wow, I thought, *he's talking to me.* It was almost like somebody had told him everything that was going on in my life. Right at that moment, I could feel God watching over me. I looked up with a smile and whispered, "Thanks, God."

Rev. Brown had more good things to say. "Finally, young people, know that all your dreams can come true. God has put them in your heart, and it's up to you to develop them. It's okay to dream of being a football player, a singer, or an actor. But, when you focus on being a star for Christ then your life will be truly rewarding."

When he was done, I sprang to my feet. I didn't clap or anything, I just stood up with everybody else. I was amazed that God was speaking to me so clearly through this message. As soon as church was over, I went up to the youth minister and told him that he did a great job.

"Thanks, young man. I hope you got something from what I said."

"Yes, sir. I did."

Later that day when we were on the plane, I squeezed Mom's hand and said, "I'm sorry I gave you a hard time. I just wanted to be like you on TV, making people smile and making the world a happier place."

"If that's really what you want, son, one day—when

the time is right—you can work to make it happen. And I accept your apology. I know you were disappointed and I'm not trying to stop any of your dreams. I just know that there is a lot that comes with the life of being a young actor. It can be great, but I think being a kid is even greater."

I reached up and kissed her cheek. I wanted her to know that I got it. Then I leaned back and prayed. *"Thank You, God, for allowing me to hear that great message today. I needed to understand that things aren't always going to be the way I want them to be, but that doesn't mean I should quit, get mad, or give up. I want to make You proud. I want to finish strong, and I want to do my best for You. Will You help me to remember that?"*

⬤ ⬤ ⬤

It was good to be home. I had to admit it. I liked Hollywood, but I loved having my own room.

The fact that Mom came back with us meant a lot too. Even though it was my birthday and school was about to start soon, I didn't need anything else. Not even back-to-school clothes. I was just happy that my family was together.

It wouldn't even matter if all we did was go out to dinner or stay home and play some games. As long as we were hanging out with each other, I would still have the best birthday present ever.

I was sitting on my bed and thinking about everything.

Then I started to pray, *"Lord, thank You, for all that You've given me. My family and even my crazy brother are all getting along. We're real good. My faith is strong, and I believe in my dreams. I'm not yet sure what I want to be when I grow up, but I know I can be whatever I put my mind to. I guess I'm growing up because I appreciate my life like never before. Most of all, I want to please You and care about other people. I want to keep working hard in school. And, like the minister in California said, I want to go the distance in everything I do."*

I didn't even get to say amen before Antoine popped into my room and said, "Man, I'd be mad if my parents didn't plan anything for my birthday. I mean, I'm glad they're gettin' along and stuff. But, today is supposed to be about you. It's your day, and it looks like it's gonna be boring."

My brother hadn't changed that much. He still liked to stir up trouble. But I wasn't going to let him sweat me. I was happy, and that was enough for me. I felt even more special when my parents walked into my room, arm-in-arm.

"Antoine, why are you trying to get your brother all riled up?" Mom asked him. She had finally caught him trying to push my buttons.

"You know we wouldn't forget to plan something for Alec's birthday."

He looked at Mom and said, "Uh, yeah, right. I don't see any plans. What are you gonna do, Mom? Go up in the attic and pull down that old party box with the hats and horns that's been up there forever?"

"Ha ha ha, Antoine, that's so funny," Mom replied. "No way."

She walked over to the window and pulled back the curtain. "Oh, my goodness, Alec, come and see!" Mom shouted happily.

I wondered what was out there and rushed over to find out what could be so special. My eyes grew wide when I spotted a long, black limousine sitting in front of our house.

"What's goin' on?" I asked.

"You ready to roll or what, son? You know, they don't just ride this way in L.A.," said Dad.

"HUH! I'm goin', right?" Antoine quickly said.

Dad just laughed at him, and said, "Boy, come on."

In a flash, Antoine and I flew down the stairs and out the front door.

When the driver opened the limo door, I had another surprise. All of my buddies were inside. Morgan had on the cutest dress I've ever seen her wear. Billy looked like he had already eaten some of my cake because icing was all over his face. Don't even ask me where he got it from. And my boy, Trey, reached out to give me a fist bump.

My family climbed in, and we headed to my favorite restaurant. I love going there. Not only did they have good food, but there were fun games to play all over the place.

When we stepped out of the limo and went inside,

Dad led us to a private room. Boy, I couldn't be more surprised. At least, that's what I thought. But when we walked in, there was Grandma Frances and her sister, Aunt Dot. I'm so glad that she's doing much better. My cousin, Lil' Pete, was sitting beside them. Right next to them was Grandma Ana. She had come all the way from Hollywood along with her brother, Uncle Jack, and his wife, Aunt Jan.

"Oh, man!" I shouted. I was grinning so hard that my face started to hurt.

When they all shouted "Happy Birthday!" I hardly knew how to respond. This was more than I could ever dream about. I didn't know the plans for my birthday, and I hadn't worried about it either. But, then I got this huge blessing. The Lord was already teaching me that it pays to trust Him and not worry about things.

Really, I would have been okay if nothing had happened for me other than my family being together. But having my extended family and my friends with me in my favorite restaurant, celebrating my eleventh birthday, was just fantastic. All I could do was give every one of them hugs.

After that, my friends pulled me away and we went to the arcade to have some fun. I dominated Billy and Trey on the racing game. Later on, my buddies told me that they took pity on me because it was my birthday. According to them, they let me win by a landslide. I don't think so.

Then Morgan asked me to play a game with her.

"You look nice," I said.

"Thanks. Did you enjoy Hollywood?"

"A lot more than I thought I would."

"Yeah, I guess it's an amazing place. I didn't think you were going to come back."

"It probably wouldn't have mattered to anybody."

"What do you mean? It would have mattered to me. You're my friend, my good friend, Alec. We help each other keep it real, and we challenge each other with our academics. It would be hard for me if you moved away. Now, come on, let's play. It's my turn to beat you," Morgan said with a smile.

And beat me she did. I don't know if her skills were just that good or if I was sidetracked by her telling me that she wouldn't like it if I moved away. What was that all about? I know I'm growing up, and I guess I'm seeing her in a different light. Morgan is really cool, and I'm glad to know that she thinks I'm cool too.

● ● ●

Later that evening, I was super excited and couldn't go to sleep. So I got out of my bed and down on my knees. I thanked God for all my blessings. When I got back up, I was startled to see Mom. She was standing in my doorway. Through the moonlight, I could see her watching me.

"You're an awesome boy, Alec London. You know, my mom and I go back tomorrow," she said, as she came over and gave me a big hug.

At that moment, I just squeezed her tight. I didn't want to let her go. We'd grown super close.

"Be careful. If you squeeze too hard, she won't be able to breathe, son," Dad said chuckling, as he stood in the doorway.

I would never do anything to hurt Mom. I just didn't want to let her go. They both understood.

"Lisa, you'd better go ahead and tell that boy."

"You mean, you're stayin', Mom?" I asked, still hopeful. She looked at Dad.

"Tell him," he said again.

"It's a compromise, honey. I'm going to come back every other week," Mom said.

"Aw, Mom, that's great news! I'm gonna get to see you more!"

"Yes, baby."

"Alec, we're so proud of you. You're smart, you're athletic, and you're growing up into a fine young man," my dad said, as he playfully jabbed me in the arm.

Mom added, "And, best of all, you love God. Keep putting Him first, baby, and your life will always have a wonderful outcome."

Letter to Mom

Dear Mom,

I want you to know that I understand your decision for me to wait before I try acting. Still, I was super happy to get a callback from the film company. Grandma is ambitious, and I also know that she has a good heart.

I want you to know that I'm willing to trust you and to wait for the right time. Most of all, I'm willing to trust God to help me go the distance in everything I do.

Your son,
Thrilled Alec

Word Search: Famous Baseball Players

Over the decades, there have been lots of famous and talented baseball players. A few standouts are Jackie Robinson, Willie Mays, Hank Aaron, and Reggie Jackson from the 60–70s, Frank Thomas and Ken Griiffey, Jr. in the 80–90s. And in the 2000s is Jimmy Rollins. Can you find their names?

```
Y  M  B  A  P  A  A  R  O  N  E  N
Q  D  S  S  N  I  L  L  O  R  S  Z
I  C  Y  V  Q  N  O  S  K  C  A  J
Q  A  U  L  Y  C  N  F  Z  E  M  E
M  V  R  G  R  I  F  F  E  Y  O  V
I  E  I  T  B  G  B  J  A  L  H  O
X  Q  E  O  T  G  Y  L  L  Q  T  P
K  D  R  C  R  V  I  V  D  X  Y  K
I  P  F  T  B  Q  S  U  L  G  L  Y
C  A  P  J  G  X  B  W  F  P  P  T
R  A  E  S  G  I  G  U  G  U  K  Z
I  G  Z  R  S  R  W  X  P  M  R  E
```

AARON (Hank)	GRIFFEY (Ken Jr.)	JACKSON (Reggie)
MAYS (Willie)	ROBINSON (Jackie)	ROLLINS (Jimmy)
THOMAS (Frank)		

Alec London Series: Book 3

GOING THE DISTANCE

Stephanie Perry Moore & Derrick Moore
Discussion Questions

1. Alec London is disappointed when his mother can't make it home for a visit. Do you think he should be upset? How do you handle things when your wishes don't come true?

2. Alec and Antoine want to relax for the summer, but their father takes them to baseball camp. Do you think Alec was right to be upset about the camp? Do you think it is okay to tell your parents when you don't want to do something?

3. Alec truly doesn't like baseball camp. Do you think it is okay for Alec to drop out of the program just because he doesn't like it? When you feel it is not easy to be part of a group, what are ways you can encourage yourself to go the distance?

4. Alec's dad can't go with the family to California. Is Alec right for being upset? When things don't go your way, how can you find the good in the situation anyway?

5. When Alec gets to Hollywood, he meets his mom's mother. His grandmother and his mother haven't been getting along. Why do you think it is good to try and get over past hurts? What are ways you can make up with someone that hurt you?

6. When the brothers try out for a commercial, Antoine really wanted the job but Alec got hired instead. Do you think Alec was right to want Antoine to take the acting job even though Alec was picked for it? Do you believe God wants you to put other people's needs before your own?

7. Alec enjoys acting and wants to keep auditioning, but his mother says he cannot at that time. Do you feel he should understand her decision to keep him from trying to become an actor? Why was Alec right to obey his mom and wait until a later time? How can you let your parents or guardian know you respect their decisions?

Social Studies Worksheet
13 Original Colonies

Use the following chart to answer the questions below.

The British Empire established 13 colonies in North America. The first colony was founded by the London Company at Jamestown, Virginia, in 1607. Listed below are other colonies, along with the year they were founded and their founding person or group.

COLONY NAME	YEAR FOUNDED	FOUNDED BY
Virginia	1607	London Company
Massachusetts	1620	Puritans
New Hampshire	1623	John Wheelwright
Maryland	1634	Lord Baltimore
Connecticut	1635	Thomas Hooker
Rhode Island	1636	Roger Williams
Delaware	1638	Peter Minuit and New Sweden Company
North Carolina	1653	Virginians
South Carolina	1663	Eight Nobles with a Royal Charter from Charles II
New Jersey	1664	Lord Berkeley and Sir George Carteret
New York	1664	Duke of York
Pennsylvania	1682	William Penn
Georgia	1732	James Edward Oglethorpe

13 Original Colonies

Questions

(1) What year was Massachusetts founded? _____

(2) What colony was founded in 1638? _____

(3) What colony did the Virginians found? _____

(4) What year was New York founded? _____

(5) Who was the founder of Georgia? _____

Science Worksheet
Science Lab Safety Procedures

When you work in a science laboratory, there are some very important rules that need to be followed before conducting your science experiment. Answer "True" or "False" to the following statements about lab safety.

1. A teacher does not have to be present when entering the lab. _____

2. Leave all your personal belongings outside the lab. _____

3. You may run in the lab to avoid accidents. _____

4. You may shout and play while conducting an experiment. _____

5. Long hair should be tied back. _____

6. Safety goggles must be worn to protect your eyes. _____

7. You may eat and drink in the laboratory. _____

8. You can wait until the end of class to clean up any spills. _____

9. You should never taste the chemicals. _____

10. Do not use chipped glassware. _____

11. Follow all instructions carefully. _____

12. Ask questions if you are uncertain about the experiment. _____

13. When you are finished with your experiment, you can leave waste materials out in your area. _____

14. You do not have to put away all your equipment or clean your work bench. _____

15. You should always wash your hands when you are done. _____

Teach Me, Coach: Baseball

So you dream of hitting the ball out of the bark, huh? Well, to be truly successful at baseball, it takes more than being able to hit a homerun. You also need to know the rules.

Baseball is a fun, intense game. Playing the sport is most enjoyable when the regulations are being followed. The rules of baseball are complex, but you can learn the basic fundamentals of the game listed below.

They are divided into five parts: (1) the playing field, (2) players, (3) game structure, (4) pitching and hitting, and (5) getting an out.

Baseball Playing Field

In baseball, the playing field is made up of an infield and an outfield. The *infield* is made up of four bases that form a square. This square is known as the *baseball diamond*. One of the bases is called *home plate* and this is where the batter stands. There is also *first base*, *second base*, and *third base*. The runners proceed to each base in order.

In the middle of the infield, there is the *pitcher's mound*. The pitcher has to have one foot on the pitcher rubber when throwing a pitch. In a standard baseball field, the distance between each base is 90 feet. The distance from the pitcher's mound to home plate is 60 feet and 6 inches. The lines that are made between home plate and first base, as well as home plate and third base are called the foul lines. These lines expand all the way to the outfield and, together with the home run fence, define baseball's *outfield*.

How many bases are there in baseball? _____

Baseball Players

The offensive positions are hitters and batters. The defensive baseball positions can be divided into three main categories: (1) the battery (2) infielders (3) outfielders. The baseball battery is made up of the pitcher and the catcher. The baseball infielders are four players: the first baseman, second baseman, shortstop, and third baseman. The baseball outfielders are the right fielder, center fielder, and left fielder.

How many people make up the baseball battery? ───────────

Baseball Game Structure

A baseball game is defined by outs and innings. A game is usually made up of 9 innings, but may be fewer innings at various levels of play. During an inning, each team takes a turn at bat. A team's turn at bat continues until there are three outs. After three outs, either the inning is over or the other team takes its turn (the home team bats at the bottom, or second half, of the inning). A run is scored for each player who safely crosses home plate, and the winner of the game is the team with the most runs at the end of the final inning. If the game is tied additional innings are played until there is a winner.

How many innings is the usual baseball game? ───────────

Baseball Pitching and Hitting

The pitcher tosses the ball over home plate in an effort to get a *strike*. A strike is when the batter does not swing at a baseball that is pitched over the area of home plate, above the batter's knees, and below the batter's belt. This is usually called the *strike zone*, but that is up to the interpretation of the umpire calling the game.

A strike also takes place when the batter swings at the baseball and misses it entirely, regardless of the location of the pitch. A strike also is called when a batter hits the ball foul. A *foul ball* only counts as a first or second strike. Any fouls after the second strike do not count as balls or strikes.

A *pitch* that is not a strike and is not swung at by the batter is called a *ball*. If the pitcher throws 4 balls, the batter gets to walk to first base. If the pitcher throws 3 strikes, the batter is out. When the batter hits the baseball within the play boundaries, the runner can proceed to the bases.

How many balls are thrown before a person gets to walk?

_____

Getting an Out

Once the batter hits the baseball in play, the batter becomes a base *runner*. The defensive team, called the fielders, try to get the base runner out before the runner can get to the base. This is called *getting an out*.

The first goal is to catch the baseball before it hits the ground. If the fielders do this, the batter is out and all other base runners must return to their original base before they are tagged, or they will be out. Once the ball touches the ground in play, then the fielders must get the baseball and try to tag base runners.

An *out* can be gained at any time there is a base runner. If a base runner tries to steal a base or has a big lead off of the base, the pitcher or catcher may be able to throw him out.

Can an out be gained any time there is a base runner?

_____

Overall, baseball is a long game. Going the distance in the game of baseball requires hard work and preparation. Don't ever forget that it will take some hard work before you can be good at hitting or catching the ball, but hard work pays off when you play this exciting game. So be determined and never give up just because the game may be tough. Just work at it even more, and one day your dream will come true. You'll be the one hitting the ball out of the park!

Chapter 1 Solution

BATTERY   **BUNT**   **CLEANUP**   **DIAMOND**

HOMERUN   **PITCH**   **RELAY**
(Home Run)

Chapter 2 Solution

P	O	W	E	R	H	I	T	T	E	R	U
I	N	A	M	E	S	A	B	N	Q	E	Y
N	C	N	C	D	B	R	E	T	I	H	G
C	C	R	A	L	W	Z	P	P	A	C	H
H	N	N	T	E	C	M	O	X	X	T	J
I	T	T	C	I	U	T	M	J	R	I	X
T	W	L	H	F	S	Z	O	O	W	P	Q
T	C	N	E	T	M	N	H	N	V	V	Z
E	G	Q	R	U	R	V	P	A	H	R	G
E	U	O	A	O	S	O	T	W	J	N	Q
R	H	D	W	E	D	L	U	F	B	X	B
S	S	W	O	V	I	P	E	N	M	O	Z

BASEMAN	CATCHER	OUTFIELDER
PINCHHITTER (Pinch Hitter)	PITCHER	POWERHITTER (Power Hitter)
SHORTSTOP		

Chapter 3 Solution

P	L	G	J	U	A	Q	W	J	G	V	J
V	G	B	C	O	P	U	R	R	B	S	M
K	L	W	D	E	G	O	O	E	A	A	L
L	E	B	W	H	W	U	R	N	U	V	G
O	L	E	L	A	N	I	R	U	L	Y	Y
N	M	A	I	D	L	O	E	S	G	F	M
A	Q	N	B	A	L	K	M	C	K	N	V
F	N	A	X	L	I	U	E	O	K	P	D
R	L	I	P	R	U	G	I	P	H	A	N
L	P	I	T	C	H	O	U	T	Y	T	E
T	J	S	J	V	N	W	F	N	T	U	G
L	X	K	O	Y	I	Z	I	B	G	V	L

BALK   **ERROR**   **FOULBALL**   **GROUNDBALL**
                      (Foul Ball)   (Ground Ball)

            PITCHOUT   **STRIKE**   **WALK**

Chapter 4 Solution

BRAVES   **CARDINALS**   **INDIANS**

PHILLIES   **RANGERS**   **RED SOX**

YANKEES

Chapter 5 Solution

ARIZONASTATE   **CLEMSON**   **OKLAHOMA**   **RICE**
(Arizona State)

SCAROLINA   **STANFORD**   **VIRGINIA**
(South Carolina)

Chapter 6 Solution

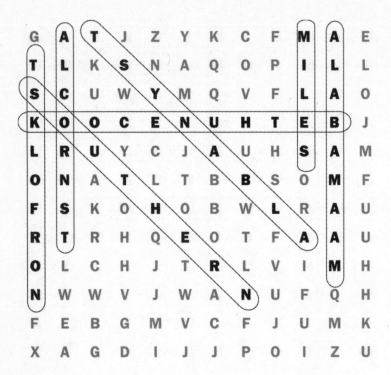

ALABAMAAM
(Alabama A&M)

ALBANYST
(Albany State)

ALCORNST
(Alcorn State)

BETHUNECOOK
(Bethune Cookman)

MILES

NORFOLKST
(Norfolk State)

SOUTHERN

Chapter 7 Solution

AARON (Hank)   **GRIFFEY (Ken Jr.)**   **JACKSON (Reggie)**

MAYS (Willie)   **ROBINSON (Jackie)**   **ROLLINS (Jimmy)**

THOMAS (Frank)

Answer Keys

13 Original Colonies

1) 1620
2) Delaware
3) North Carolina
4) 1664
5) James Edward Oglethorpe

Teach Me Coach: Baseball

1) 4 bases
2) 2 people
3) 9 innings
4) 4 balls
5) yes

Science Lab Safety Procedures

1) FALSE
2) TRUE
3) FALSE
4) FALSE
5) TRUE
6) TRUE
7) FALSE
8) FALSE
9) TRUE
10) TRUE
11) TRUE
12) TRUE
13) FALSE
14) FALSE
15) TRUE

ACKNOWLEDGMENTS

Well, it's the end of the school year at the Moore home. All three of our kids are busy completing projects, turning in final work, and studying for exams. Though they've had a great school year, it's not over until it's over. That means they have to finish strong or grades could drop.

This lesson is one that can help anyone succeed in every part of life. Don't ever give up. Keep going, and don't stop until the goal is reached. If you give your best, you'll reach the prize. And we hope this novel blesses every reader and inspires each one to go the distance.

We have a lot of people to thank, especially our dear friends Antonio and Gloria London and their family, who inspired us with the main character's last name.

For our parents, Dr. Franklin and Shirley Perry, and Ann Redding, we can keep going because of your support. Thanks for giving us your all.

For our Moody/Lift Every Voice Books team, especially

Karen Waddles, we can keep inspiring others in print because you believe in us. Thanks for going the distance in publishing and not giving up on the Lift Every Voice Books imprint.

For our Georgia Tech family, especially Coach Paul and Susan Johnson, we can make a difference because of your solid support. Thank you for having us on your team.

For our assistants, Ciara Roundtree and Alyxandra Pinkston, we can go on to finish a project because we have your help. Thank you for fitting us into all you've got going on.

For our dear friends, Calvin Johnson, Tashard Choice, Chett and Lakeba Williams, Dennis and Leslie Perry, Clayton and Kelly Ivey, Jay and Debbie Spencer, Randy Roberts, John Rainey, Peyton Day, Jim and Deen Sanders, Bobby and Sarah Lundy, Sid Callaway, Dicky Clark, Danny Buggs, Patrick and Krista Nix, Byron and Kim Johnson, Jenell Clark, Carol Hardy, Sid Callaway, Nicole Smith, Jackie Dixon, Harry and Torian Colon, Brett and Loni Perriman, Byron and Kim Forest, Vickie Davis, Brock White, Jamell Meeks, Michele Jenkins, Christine Nixon, Danny Buggs, Lois Barney, Veronica Evans, Sophia Nelson, Laurie Weaver, Byrant and Taiwanna Brown-Bolds, Deborah Thomas, Yolanda Rodgers-Howsie, Dayna Fleming, Denise Gilmore, Thelma Day, Adrian Davis, and Donald and Deborah Bradley, we have richer lives because you're there. You are all dear to our hearts. Thank you for caring for the Moore family.

For our son, Dustyn, and oldest daughter, Sydni, we

keep going because of our love for you. Thank you for going the distance in all you do.

For our new young readers, we pray you all keep going and going and going, until you reach your dreams. Thank you so much for reading this novel.

And for our heavenly Father, we'll keep going for You until you call us home. Thank You for allowing us to enjoy seventeen years of wedded bliss.

ALEC LONDON SERIES

978-0-8024-0411-4

978-0-8024-0410-7

978-0-8024-0412-1   978-0-8024-0414-5   978-0-8024-0413-8

The Alec London books are chapter books written for boys, 8–12 years old. Alec London is introduced in Stephanie Perry Moore's previously released series Morgan Love. In this new series, readers get a glimpse of Alec's life up close and personal. The series provides moral lessons that will aid in character development, teaching boys how to effectively deal with the various issues they face at this stage of life. The books will also help boys develop their English and math skills as they read through the stories and complete the entertaining and educational exercises provided at the end of each chapter and in the back of the book.

L E V B
LIFT EVERY VOICE BOOKS

LiftEveryVoiceBooks.com
MoodyPublishers.com

ALSO RANS SERIES

The Also Rans series is written for boys, ages 8-12. This series enourages youth, especially young boys, to give all they got in everything they do and never give up.

978-0-8024-2253-8

RUN, JEREMIAH, RUN

As a foster child, life for Jeremiah is a garbage bag filled with his things, a new school, and worst of all, finding a new family. Jeremiah holds on to his grandmother's promise of a handful of mustard seeds being planted one day to grow into a tree of his own. After being expelled from school again, he thinks that no one will want him to be a part of their family. With the help of his friends, he learns about teamwork and what it means to persevere.

978-0-8024-2259-0

COMING ACROSS JORDAN

When Jordan and brother Kevin decide to paint a mural (which is really graffiti) on the school's property, they get in trouble. They learn, along with their good friend Melanie, the lesson that even in using their talents to do something good, they have to pay attention and not break the rules.

L E V B
LIFT EVERY VOICE BOOKS

LiftEveryVoiceBooks.com
MoodyPublishers.com

MORGAN LOVE SERIES

978-0-8024-2263-7

978-0-8024-2264-4

978-0-8024-2267-5   978-0-8024-2266-8   978-0-8024-2265-1

The Morgan Love series is a chapter book series written for girls, 7–9 years old. The books provide moral lessons that will aid in character development. They will also help young girls develop their vocabulary, English, and math skills as they read through the stories and complete the entertaining and educational exercises provided at the end of each chapter and in the back of the book.

L E V B
LIFT EVERY VOICE BOOKS

LiftEveryVoiceBooks.com
MoodyPublishers.com

Lift Every Voice Books

Lift every voice and sing
Till earth and heaven ring,
Ring with the harmonies of Liberty;
Let our rejoicing rise
High as the listening skies,
Let it resound loud as the rolling sea.
Sing a song full of the faith that the dark past has taught us,
Sing a song full of the hope that the present has brought us,
Facing the rising sun of our new day begun
Let us march on till victory is won.

The Black National Anthem, written by James Weldon Johnson in 1900, captures the essence of Lift Every Voice Books. Lift Every Voice Books is an imprint of Moody Publishers that celebrates a rich culture and great heritage of faith, based on the foundation of eternal truth—God's Word. We endeavor to restore the fabric of the African-American soul and reclaim the indomitable spirit that kept our forefathers true to God in spite of insurmountable odds.

We are Lift Every Voice Books—Christ-centered books and resources for restoring the African-American soul.

For more information on other books and products
written and produced from a biblical perspective, go to
www.lifteveryvoicebooks.com or write to:

Lift Every Voice Books
820 N. LaSalle Boulevard
Chicago, IL 60610
www.lifteveryvoicebooks.com